The Darkness Rising

DAVID STUART DAVIES

CONTENTS

THE DARKNESS RISING
A Supernatural Thriller

ONE

Kate stared out at the grey mist rolling in from the sea. It moved on the faint chill breeze, coiling its tentacles around objects in its path. Soon it would envelop the little cottage like a shroud, pressing its moist breath against the windows, holding her in its thrall. Already the trees, which five minutes ago had been distinct silhouettes, were now just vague spectral shadows fingering the growing gloom.

Kate gave an involuntary shudder; and yet somehow she welcomed the mist, welcomed its isolating protection. The longer she could keep the world at a distance, out of focus, a blur, so much the better.

The old kitchen clock whirred and struck the hour, breaking the ticking quiet. She gave a little start at the noise and then smiled at her own uneasiness.

Michael.

His name came to her again. From out of nowhere. It just slipped unbidden into her consciousness. But then, it never really left her. It lay crouched in some corner of her mind like a spider, waiting for an opportunity to scuttle out.

Michael.

It wasn't surrender exactly; it was simply that she had no defence against its power. She couldn't fight it or maybe she didn't want to. Once again, she found to her surprise and annoyance warm tears on her face. For a moment she held still, closing her eyes, pressing the lids tightly shut.

'Michael'.

She said his name softly and slowly, like a child who makes a secret wish or tries to break a magic curse.

***

'And for God's sake, don't be late for the script conference on Monday. Parker's got something pretty big up his sleeve.'

'His secretary claims another location,' grinned David, hastily cramming papers into his briefcase.

Rob Moore's expression softened slightly, his square features shifting into a smile. Brief and polite. 'I mean it, David. I've had these dastardly emails before and they always mean big trouble. Formal and sinister they are. Take a look.' He thrust the printout under David's nose. 'You mark my words: a 'death' is imminent.'

David read Parker's memo:

'FOR THE ATTENTION OF:

Rob Moore, script co-ordinator

VERNON & SONS

Special script panel meeting for Monday 10th–10.30 Prompt

Agenda: Discuss falling ratings, possible remedies.

Please inform all script panel members.

NELSON PARKER Head of Popular Drama L.T.V.'

'Whose death did you have in mind?' asked David passing the memo back to Rob.

He shrugged his huge shoulders. 'It's not for me to say, but if I had my way, I'd kill off that cow, Vera Cooper.'

'Oh come now, Rob,' said David, 'I believe I hear the gentle sound of sour grapes being trodden. Just because our dear Vera gave your come on the brush off, there's no need to go around arranging a massive overdose of Valium for her.'

Rob grinned, eyes sparking with wicked merriment. 'Crushed by a runaway juggernaut is what I had in mind. Lots of blood and Geordie screaming. Might even have her bloody wig fly off.'

'You are heartless bastard,' said David lightly, returning the grin, before grabbing his coat and heading for the door. 'Besides,' he added, turning to throw Rob an afterthought, 'Vera adds sex appeal to the show. All those tight sweaters with the generous flash of cleavage must do something for the ratings. If you're going to bump someone off, I reckon Sir Thomas Vernon is your man. Important character in the firm, big funeral, reshuffle in the board room, family squabbles over the will—plenty of mileage.'

Rob frowned. 'It's an idea, but it'd be a bit tough on old Rex Mulligan.'

'It'll be tough on whoever gets the chop, but that's showbiz. One minute you're heading a thriving family business twice weekly in all regions and the next you're down the job centre to see if they want any extras for a laxative commercial.'

'You'll go far in television, David Cole. You've got the two main qualities required: a quick brain and a cold heart.'

'Hark at the man. And who was it wanted to squash our dear Vera?'

'On second thoughts, how about her being savaged by a rabid pack of Rottweilers?' He chuckled to himself and then heaved a sigh. 'Come on, David, let's drift off and have a few drinks and put this sordid world a little out of focus.'

'Not tonight, Rob. I'm going down to the cottage. Anyway, perhaps we'll both need it more after Monday's session.'

'Maybe', he sighed and then after a thought he grimaced and nodded decisively. 'Definitely!'

David glanced at his watch. 'Look, I've got to be off. I want to get there before it gets really dark.'

'OK. See you. How is Kate by the way?'

David's face clouded. 'I don't really know. She worries me.'

***

Michael.

Kate cradled a cup of coffee in her hands, the warmth of it strangely comforting as she peered out of the window at the mist, which now completely obliterated the view of the sea and most of the garden. In the stillness she could hear the breakers, but they seemed so far away, like distant strange whispers belonging to another world.

It was somehow reassuring to stare at the shimmering, shifting leaden wall. There was nothing precise, nothing definite out there—just an intangible greyness. From the dull convoluted grey coils she fashioned shapes like a child who picks out faces in the patterns of wallpaper. Smokey lions prowled and stalked invisible prey out there, while bushes, root-free it seemed, floated wildly in the air.

And there were man-shapes, too. Well, one man-shape.

Michael.

At that thought, Kate turned instinctively away from the window. Her eyes darting around the room, seeking refuge. They finally rested on the kitchen clock. David would be here soon. However, somehow this thought did not cheer her. His arrival wouldn't actually solve anything. Like the isolation of the cottage, he was just another of her ploys for keeping reality at bay.

Irresistibly, she found her gaze drawn back to the grey world beyond the glass.

The man-shape was still there.

She turned away abruptly. Better check the oven timer.

And the central heating thermostat. It seemed cooler now.

***

They had been let down on purpose, he was sure of that. One, even two flat tyres could be seen as Old Mother Fate kicking you in the crutch, but not all four. Which nasty bastard had it in for him so much?

David kicked one of the wheels and cursed. Now he really would be late and Kate would not like that. He tried ringing her on his mobile with no success. The bloody internet connection at the cottage was as unreliable as a fairground goldfish.

With a muttered expletive, he opened the boot and reached for the foot pump.

***

Kate continued to busy herself with minor chores for another ten minutes. Mechanical habit led her through the routines while her mind was fixed elsewhere.

Michael.

When at last she'd finished, she knew she would have to go back to the window. It was like a magnet to her. Despite the reluctant nagging at the back of her mind, she wanted to go back. Indeed, she needed to. The temptation was too great.

It was with a mixture of disappointment and relief that she saw that there was nothing there. The glaucous shapes had gone, exorcised by the gentle breeze. But her first glance had lied to her, deceived her in order to protect her. As her eyes focused on the dark world beyond the glass, she did see something there. In the centre of the garden it stood, blacker and more distinct than the other shapes had been: it was that solitary man-shape.

Michael.

She snatched at the empty coffee cup. Must wash this up, she told herself. Her grasp was shaky; the cup slipped from her hand and fell to the floor. She gave a soft gasp of despair as the noise of the smashing cup pierced the silence like a scream, the fragments skating in all directions.

Yet she did not move. And neither did the shape.

Or did it?

Was there some subtle, gentle undulating movement, or was it just the eddies of mist around the shape? Around it? What was she thinking? It was the mist—a part, an element of it.

But no. It was moving. To hell with logic: it was moving. The thick grey tendrils rose and fell in a regular motion as thought it was attempting to communicate with her. Kate's hand flew to her mouth and she issued a brief sob as though the worst, and yet the inevitable, had happened. The grey intangible thing out there was actually beckoning her to join it.

***

By the time the credits were rolling to the accompaniment of the faintly martial theme tune concluding another episode of 'Vernon & Sons', Matron was already asleep. It was a regular occurrence. She used the programme as a means of stimulating her fatigue resulting from a long day dealing with a series of schoolboy ailments from boils to bronchitis.

'Vernon & Sons' held no interest for her apart from its soporific qualities and she hardly survived more than five minutes into the episode before her flickering eyelids lowered, finally surrendering to sleep. It was better and indeed healthier than sleeping tablets. However, her awakening was more erratic. Sometimes she would doze on for an hour, at other times the changing rhythm of sound brought about by the brash commercials which followed 'Vernon & Sons' would disturb her sleep pattern and ease her into consciousness. On this occasion, however, her arousal was far more abrupt and disturbing. It was precipitated by a sequence of loud, insistent staccato knocks on her study door; these were accompanied by several, almost frantic calls to her.

With a sigh of resignation, Matron retrieved her discarded shoes from under her chair, snapped off the television and opened the door. There she found Collier, one of the senior prefects, in a state of agitation.

'Matron, come quickly.'

'What is it, Collier? Is the school on fire?'

'It's Barlow. Tim Barlow, one of the lads in my dormitory. I think he's having a fit.'

***

When Matron reached the dormitory, she found that Barlow was being held down on his bed by four of the bigger boys, while the rest, white-faced and silent, stood at a distance, watching uneasily.

Timothy Barlow was a small, dark-haired boy with fine, delicate, almost feminine features and an unnaturally pale complexion. As Matron approached his bedside, the boy's contortions lessened but he still continued to twist his head from side to side, his eyes rolling so wildly that, intermittently, only the whites were visible. Froth collected at the corners of his mouth as he muttered unintelligibly.

'Leave him be,' Matron instructed the boys who had been holding him down. They did as she ordered and the she bent over him and held his head still. She felt his forehead: it was ice-cold.

'Timothy. Timothy.' She spoke in soft, soothing tones, the like of which most of the boys had never her use before. They exchanged surprised glances, but no one dared utter a word. She was quietly confident there was no real problem here. He wasn't the first pupil in her charge to suffer an epileptic fit. If she could calm him, he would be back to normal within five minutes, probably remembering nothing of the attack. All she had to be sure of was that he didn't swallow his tongue.

'Timothy, can you hear me?' She gently ran her fingers over his forehead. 'All is well. Just breathe deeply. Relax. Simply relax.'

Her voice was soft but persuasive and after a few moments his body grew less agitated and the features less tense.

Matron stroked the boy's cheek. 'That's right, Timothy. Just relax. Let the demon go.'

He gazed at her in wonder at these words and then his body suddenly became limp. For a moment he lay still and then slowly he turned to face her, his eyes widening with apparent recognition, a smile touching his lips. It was a very unpleasant smile.

'You are all right now, Timothy. You are back with us once more,' Matron cooed.

With a sudden fierce effort, the boy pulled himself free of her restraint and sat up on the bed facing her. 'Kate,' he whispered; but the voice that issued from his lips was not that of a ten year old child, but the deep bass tones of a mature adult. 'Kate, my darling,' the voice said again.

And then without warning, Timothy Barlow flung his arms around Matron's neck, and pulling her to him, he kissed her with force and passion. His lips slid smoothly on to hers and his tongue penetrated her mouth.

With a cry of disgust, Matron thrust the boy from her back onto the bed, where, like a deflated balloon, he collapsed into a dead faint.

***

Kate pulled the raincoat further round her shoulders, for the evening was really chilly and the mist, clammy and moist, pressed against her face. Despite being outside, away from the confines of the cottage, she began to feel claustrophobic.

What the hell was she doing in the garden anyway?

Michael.

The click of her heels on the path echoed like some eerie Morse code. The light from the kitchen window projected a faint golden rectangle onto the lawn. Straining her eyes, she peered beyond it into the undulating grey whorls for the strange man-shape she has glimpsed when inside.

It was still there, but it had retreated and now hovered, or so it seemed, at the edge of the lawn. Kate knew she was crazy to be out there at all, but she astounded herself by actually addressing the vague, animated fragment of darkness.

'Don't go,' she whispered with some urgency and then added tentatively and tenderly 'Michael?'

For an instant the mist shifted and cleared around the figure. It raised a ghostly arm and beckoned to her. Instinctively, she moved forward, feeling her feet squelch softly into the wet lawn. The figure remained. It was waiting now. Waiting for her.

***

The Goddamn roads had never been so busy!

David cursed silently and gripped the steering wheel in frustration as some incompetent, half-witted, geriatric buffoon in front of him chugged along at thirty miles per hour, hugging the centre of the road for comfort.

David glanced at the clock on the dashboard. Six-fifty. He was late.

Some suicidal maniac, with headlights on full beam and horn blasting, pulled by him and swerved out into the opposite lane to pass the bloody slow coach arsehole who, on seeing this dangerous manoeuvre, panicked and braked hard. To avoid a collision, David had to follow suit. He hit the brake pedal and he jerked forward, banging his head on the windscreen.

'Shit!' he cried.

Angry horns and flashing headlights from the rear prevented him from examining the extent of the damage to his forehead from where a thin trickle of blood now ran. He quickly started the car up again, clicking his seat belt in this time and he was soon in line again behind the geriatric snail. David glanced into the driving mirror to catch sight of his wound and for one chilling moment he thought the face staring back at him was not his own.

***

Kate held out her hand.

'Michael, it is you, isn't it?'

There was no reply.

Of course, there could be no reply. This was sheer madness. She had better stop now before she completely cracked up. It was all her overworked imagination playing tricks with the fog.

No. That was not quite true. Really, she wanted it to happen. It would be like an absolution. If only she could explain to him...

As she stood there, shivering in the cold grey night she admitted the truth to herself for the first time since she had learned of Michael's death. She felt pain and guilt. It was the guilt, like a locked door, which prevented her from moving forwards in her life. If only she could exorcise this guilt. Face up to it. If only she knew how. It needed more than courage. However, there really was only one way to break free from the shadow of the past, one impossible way: she needed to talk to Michael. To explain.

But he was dead.

The figure seemed to shift slightly.

'Michael, it is you, isn't it?' she found herself saying, despite being aware how ridiculous it was. Ridiculous and crazy.

They were just empty words into empty air. What on earth was she expecting? For Michael's ghost to emerge through the folds of the mist and forgive her?

'You fool,' she snapped angrily at herself and turned quickly towards the house, but something stopped her dead. Something that chilled her to the bone. Something that squeezed her heart in an icy grasp. It was that on the clammy night air, faintly but clearly, she heard that familiar dark voice calling to her.

'Kate. My darling, Kate.'

TWO

David ran into the mist about a mile from the cottage. The Audi slid smoothly into it like a hand into a thick grey glove. Another bloody delay. He cursed again and reduced speed.

The tightness he felt throughout his whole body, the tension of straining nerves dismayed David. It wasn't like him and he didn't want it to be like him. Despite his feelings—and that word would have to do for the moment—despite his feelings for Kate, he'd never been really fully at ease since he'd known her.

This affair was different, and the difference was somehow menacing to him. It threatened his comfortable, secure, untroubled bachelor world. At the age of thirty four, he had survived his twenties with barely a scrape. A few flesh wounds maybe, he told himself with a smile. There had been some serious skirmishes in the early days, but these had served as important lessons, alerting him to future pitfalls. He had seen his friends all eventually succumb to the temptation of marriage. Why, for fuck's sake, in this day and age? Who the hell needs the legal stranglehold of marriage? Was it, he wondered, that long established middle class urge for respectability, the temptation of conformity which follows the standard period of wild oating? One must obey the unwritten rules of marrying— or shacking up together at least and then procreating. Children—the extra shackle. Indeed a few of his friends had married, divorced and like some marital kamikaze were about to do it again.

David saw marriage as an unnecessary intrusion and a complication. He was honest enough with himself to admit that he was too selfish to share his life with someone else on a permanent basis. Love could never be that great. In his naïve salad days, there had been what he supposed had been real love

11

in his life, but not lately, not within vivid memory. Besides, he had been moderately successful as a writer in television and his emotions and nervous spirit had been poured into that, leaving behind a somewhat cold shell. Perhaps that is unfair. David was not cold. Kate could never have been attracted to a cold man. Rather, he was like the scripts he wrote: warm, lively and intriguing on the surface, but rather empty beneath. What had Rob Moore said of him? 'A quick brain and a cold heart.' Rob Moore was no fool.

But David did care for Kate. At least he thought he did. His feelings for her were new to him and he was unable to give them a name—or he was too frightened to. He was concerned for her, certainly. Dammit, she gave him reason! And maybe in his own way, he did love her. For who are we to define what love is for others? We do, of course, because arrogance knows no bounds, and yet we are wrong.

It would be true to say, however, that if David could now have the choice, he would have preferred never to have met Kate. But he had.

It was eighteen months ago now.

They had met in the television studio canteen. An actor friend of his was doing a drama with Kate and he introduced them.

Boy meets girl.

She had a lovely, haunting face. He adored her lips: they were wide and fleshy.

And from the first desultory lunch-time conversation, feebly supported by the shaky timbers of polite platitudes, it had all begun. Another meeting, by chance, this time on their own told them they were interested in each other. It was as simple and instant as that. He was fascinated by her quiet intelligent sexuality; she by his lively warmth. He was so unlike Michael.

One night after work he invited her for a drink. She accepted. It was an innocent, friendly invitation from one colleague to another. But they both knew that it meant more than this. They knew a significant barrier had been crossed.

David found her irresistible. She was slim and elegant with a face that radiated sensitivity and a kind of refined sensuality. He realised then that he had desired her the instant that they had met.

Initially the conversation centred on their television projects: layered small talk. It was, David mused, like an adolescent charade. 'How's it going? The show?' he asked, cradling his wine glass.

Kate wrinkled her nose. It was an eloquent gesture, but she qualified it. 'OK. It's a bit heavy in the emotion department. I'm constantly trying to tone it down while Jack... Jack Carey, you know the director...?'

David nodded and smiled.

'Well, he keeps wanting to push me over the top.'

'Perhaps he was expecting a Lady Macbeth.'

'I think he's done too many commercials and forgotten what real life is like.'

They both grinned at each other and stared gently into their drinks. The inconsequentialities were drying up.

How long was this trivial tittle tattle going to last, David asked himself. Was it up to him to strip away the formalities and get to the point? They both deserved, and in fact needed, more honesty. Surely she could feel the undercurrents, the sexual stirrings below the still waters of the conventional chatter. It wasn't just his imagination, was it? He fancied her and she would not be here swilling wine if the feeling was not mutual, would she? A man and woman, almost strangers, did not meet like this unless there was an ulterior motive. He couldn't have got it wrong, could he?

'Thanks for coming for a drink with me,' he said softly, without looking at her. There was a pause and her lips parted into a broad smile, but when she saw that he was not smiling, it quickly faded.

'We're being foolish aren't we?' he said.

'Are we?'

'Playing games like this.'

She raised an eyebrow.

'Polite games,' he reaffirmed.

'I don't think I know what you mean.'

He gave her a soft grin and a gentle shake of the head. 'And you're still playing. Does that mean, Kate, that you daren't admit it even to yourself.'

Her eyes darkened and flickered with what seemed irritation. She placed her glass down on the table in a sharp deliberate fashion, a splash of red wine slipping over the rim. Ah, I've gone too far, too quickly, David told himself. You've blown it, boy.

'I'm tired, David. I have an early call in the morning. I think I'd better be going.' She made to get up and leave, but instinctively he grabbed her hand and pulled her back. It had come to the crunch now and he didn't know what to say. All that came into his mind was second hand dialogue, the sort he wrote for his soap operas. But it was Kate who spoke.

'I'm sorry, David, it's my fault. You needn't say anything. I know.' She squeezed his hand. 'I feel it, too. But I was wrong to come. I wasn't thinking straight. We must... forget it.'

'But if the feeling is mutual?'

'There are other considerations.'

He knew of the marriage: that didn't put him off. He'd had married girlfriends before. They were often the best. Anyway, he'd heard that Kate's marriage was rather shaky. Apparently her husband was a bit of a bastard.

She got up to leave.

'Kate.'

She turned briefly.

'I'm sorry,' he said.

'So am I.' The words were a whisper; and then she was gone.

***

The headmaster fiddled with his pencil, tapping erratically on the desk. Doctor Anderton waited patiently for a response. None came. Anderton gave a polite cough. The head glanced in his direction, screwing his face into a prolonged contortion, but yet he did not speak.

Anderton repeated himself. 'I really think the parents ought to be informed.'

'Yes. Yes. So you said,' the head muttered with great irritation. 'But tonight?'

'I am afraid so. There's no certainty which way the boy will go. His condition could deteriorate rapidly overnight.'

Holding the pencil between his two hands as though testing its strength, the head gazed out of the window. From the night-blackened panes, his own reflection stared back at him like a disembodied skull. 'As I understand it, Doctor, the boy's in some sort of self-induced trance and will...' He turned to face Anderton. 'And will, we hope, come out of it naturally. Surely, in such a state his condition cannot worsen?'

Anderton allowed himself a sigh. 'The coma has, I believe, been self-induced by hysteria and will run its course with the boy regaining consciousness naturally. However, this is a dark area and there are no certainties. There is no assurance in this matter. I really believe that he needs specialised attention and the parents ought to be informed.'

The pencil snapped.

'Very well. If you organise the medical side, I will ring the boy's parents.' The head made no attempt to disguise his irritation.

'Parent, actually,' said Matron as she moved into the pool of brighter light spilled by the head's table lamp. 'His father is dead.'

***

Michael. Michael. Michael. She made a haven out of his name. Here she lounged, stretched, melted, becoming something other than herself. She felt devoured, encompassed by the dark and it was good. But not yet complete. Her body ached in the damp void, anticipating, desiring the contact. She needed it.

'Michael'. She swooped on the breath of her cry, her mouth dry with expectation, her body throbbing with excitement. She licked her lips, a shining tongue trailing a saliva path across them.

Her body tensed, offering itself to the presence.

***

Doctor Anderton entered the sick room. It was illuminated by one bright bedside lamp which threw grotesque shadows across the high flaky ceiling. Matron was gazing down at the boy with an expression which contained a mixture of shock and concern.

'Everything all right? Has there been any change?' Anderton asked tentatively.

Matron stared blankly at him for a few moments.

'What is it?' he asked, realising that something was wrong.

'This,' she said, quietly, pulling back the bedclothes from the inert form of the eight year old boy. Anderton saw, protruding from the boy's pyjamas, a large, mature and fully erect penis.

***

David's car scrunched up the gravel drive to a halt. He leapt out and made for the cottage, when his attention was arrested by some movement in the front garden. In an area of suffused yellow illumination created by the light from the kitchen window, he saw what appeared to be two figures on the lawn. They were close together almost merging into one.

Moving nearer, he thought they must be fighting. He was just about to call out when the words died in his throat. With a shudder of fear, he realised one of the figures was Kate.

***

When it came, it was cold. Deathly cold. The thrust was fierce; there was no gentleness. But then there never had been.

She gasped in pain. But it was good. Oh, it was good.

Good.

Good.

More.

Michael, more. More. Michael, more. More! More! More!

***

'Kate!' David found his voice. 'Kate!' he cried, her name echoing in the misty darkness.

***

'Fuck,' said the little boy in bed.

***

The numbness of throbbing pain, the pain that gnaws away inside, was just about to consume Kate when she heard her name floating out on the breeze. Was that sound real? Had she conjured it from her subconscious? But there it was again, more distinct—and yet, paradoxically, indistinct—muffled, protected from clarity. By the fog? The fog. Turning her head slowly to face the direction from which her name came, she scanned her surroundings like a drunk trying to recognise friends' faces at a party. Gradually she was able to make out David's vague shape at the top of the garden behind her. With a struggle, she managed to bring his name to mind, almost as a test of recognition. And then in a fragile whisper she spoke his name out loud.

That was the release. Warmth flooded back. The tension, the ache, the unreal, heightened senses faded in an instant.

***

As David rushed through the swirls of fog towards the agonised face of Kate, he realised he had been wrong. There was no one else there.

By the time he reached her, she had collapsed on to the soggy turf, a terrified grin marking her face.

THREE

Another part of the forest.

Rob Moore stirred. The blue moonlight fell across his tired face, forehead frowning in unpleasant dreams. Fiona, thin, sexless, Fiona lay stiffly by his side, unmoved by dreams or the moonlight. Sleep did not refresh Fiona, but provided her with the most treasured moments of the day: the time when she was completely unassailable, utterly private behind those closed lids and her thick cold skin.

Rob awoke to his dream.

Shadows rippled along the walls of the room, which in fact wasn't a room any longer but a pale blue seascape. The bed was afloat, shifting gently to the motion of the lapping water. This seemed less strange to Rob than the fact that he was now alone in the bed: Fiona had gone. Where? Overboard? Had she slipped unnoticed into the warm blue waters? There was no sense of loss or panic, just mild curiosity. Casually, he trailed his hand in the silky water, its warmth filtering into the rest of his body.

How relaxing.

How soporific.

The body surrendered to sleep. But one can't go to sleep in a dream, can one? A lazy smile touched his face as he considered this anomaly, his eyelids fluttering heavily. Why worry? One could drift on like this for ever, gently rocking... the warmth oozing... so soothing... Total calm.

And then...!

And then from below the warm, azure water, a thick, slimy hand took hold of his and gripped it tightly. In cold shock, Rob gave a cry of alarm. He gazed in horror at the claw-like fingers that dug into his flesh. He squirmed in heart-stopping panic, while the bed rocked, water spilling over the sides. He tried to pull his hand free from the cold clammy grasp of... of that thing below the surface. He felt his own fingers stiffen and go limp, but they did not escape from that terrible grip. Then he realised with horror that he was being pulled gradually towards the very edge of the bed, towards the warm, blue water...

With heart stopping terror, he realised what was happening. The thing means to pull me under—to drown me! The thought thundered in his brain.

He writhed on the bed, tugging, pulling, straining to free his hand. To no avail. Slowly, inexorably, Rob felt his body slither nearer the water... nearer the thing beneath its gently undulating surface.

He opened his mouth to scream but no sound issued forth. Fool! he told himself. This is a dream: you can't scream. And even if you can, who can help you in a dream? But if this is a dream, why the hell am I so terrified?

He now lay face down on the bed, his free hand grasping the edge of the mattress, while the whole of his other arm and shoulder were disappearing under the water—the warm, blue, salty water. He knew now there was no escape, there was no hope... He was doomed. Soon he would vanish for ever into the depths of his dream ocean. The water lapped against his face and he tasted the saltiness on his tongue. His body now felt numb as the underwater thing tugged harder.

He could not resist, could not fight against what he now realised was the inevitable. Rob Moore's head slipped beneath the waves and there he came face to face with the creature that had dragged him down to its saltwater embrace. There with white grinning visage, wrinkled with prolonged submersion and eyeless as a skull was a face he knew.

From her cold, barren, dreamless sleep, Fiona Moore was assailed by the screams of a madman. As consciousness propelled her back into the world, she had a vague impression of seeing her husband lying half out of bed and calling out someone's name at the top of his voice.

**

19

David had only just laid Kate on the sofa in front of the fire when the telephone rang.

'Damn! Now the bloody thing works,' he growled. For some moments he stood transfixed, caught between the need to attend to Kate and answer the insistent ring. Decisively, he strode to the phone and switched it off. Like a blessing, silence descended on the cottage. David shivered involuntarily. And then with speed, he grabbed a blanket, a bottle of brandy and a couple of glasses and returned to the sofa. Covering Kate's still inert form with the blanket, he gazed down at her pale, beautiful features and once more felt that strange tingling within him, a tenderness for her which he could not fully explain. He bent and kissed her fully on her cool lips. She stirred, eyelids fluttering, mouth moving. He kissed her again: this time she responded, and he felt her arms slip from the blanket and around his shoulders. The kiss finished, she pulled away from him and, with sleepy eyes, she tried to focus on his face.

'David?' she said softly, tentatively.

The note of surprise and uncertainty in her voice chilled him.

'Yes,' he said gently.

'Oh.'

She pulled herself up on the sofa. 'What happened?' she asked.

'You tell me. I arrived to find you having some sort of fainting fit in the garden.'

'The garden,' she said and looked beyond him. 'The garden. Yes, I was in the garden.' She closed her eyes and shuddered as though some terrible memory came to haunt her mind. Suddenly she leaned forward, throwing her arms around him. 'Oh, David, hold me...'

David did as she asked, his heart chilled. She was frightened and that meant only one thing: Michael.

***

Timothy Barlow sat up in bed. Although it was dark, he knew he wasn't in his dormitory. Where was he? His head felt strange—dry as though all the liquid had been drained out of it.

He tried to pull himself out of bed, but he found he was too weak. With a moan, he fell back on his pillow.

At the far end of the room, a solid block of yellow light slid into the darkness as the door opened. Caught in the doorway was a bulky silhouette. With grim determination, Tim raised himself on one elbow. His head throbbed. The dark shape advanced towards him, silently and with unnatural speed.

'Dad?' he asked softly. 'Dad?'

He sensed a cool hand on his feverish forehead and the strong smell of stale tobacco.

'Don't worry, Timothy, everything's going to be all right.'

The voice was familiar. It squeezed its way into his consciousness, lubricating the dry convolutions of his brain.

'Just lie back and rest for now,' came the soothing tones again. From a thousand years ago, he recognised it. It was the voice of Matron.

And then he remembered more.

Not everything but he remembered feeling ill and the cold sensation that had ebbed through his body. He remembered the strange ache between his legs. What did it all mean?

'Just rest now, Timothy, and in the morning everything will be fine.' She sounded strangely happy and filled with relief. In the darkness, he could hear the smile in her voice.

'...in the morning everything will be fine.' The phrase resounded in his brain. It was what his mother used to tell him before he came to this place. She said it nearly every night after... what happened.

And then without warning, sleep, gentle untroubled sleep, snatched him away before he could dwell on that particular thought. Matron gazed down at the little boy. His features were calm and peaceful.

Thank God, she thought. He was going to be all right.

'Thank God,' she said out loud and then shivered as though someone had walked over her grave.

***

21

Rob Moore sat, his coffee still steaming and untouched in his hand, watching the dawn seep into the sky. The warmth of the mug was comforting. He knew he couldn't go back to bed: the nightmare had put paid to any more sleep that night. He couldn't understand it - he just didn't have nightmares. Living was bad enough! Even as a kid he never suffered from troubled dreams, but the vividness of this one had really frightened him. In an attempt to shrug off the experience, he attempted a cynical smile, but his face muscles seemed to reject the idea and he didn't quite make it. It was ridiculous that a man of his age and intelligence should succumb to the drink-inspired ramblings of his unconscious. Indeed, it was ridiculous.

But he did not want to fall asleep again now.

He daren't.

So he watched and waited for the dawn. As he did so, subliminal images of the nightmare flashed inside his head, causing him to blink and to squeeze the coffee mug even harder. The thing that really frightened him was… the thing: that face, death-white, wrinkled and eyeless which had loomed close to him in the depths of his nightmare ocean. He freeze-framed that monstrous visage in his mind. There could be no doubt about it—that face belonged to Michael. Michael Barlow.

Michael.

Michael Barlow.

'Michael Barlow,' he said softly and strangely; as he did so, he felt his body relax as though by admitting the recognition and then speaking the name, the curse had been lifted from him. For the moment, at least.

At long last he took a sip of the coffee which by now was tepid and tasted awful. He felt the liquid splash down his throat and he began to feel more at ease. He stretched and yawned. The kitchen clock was clearly visible now as daylight pushed away the grey shreds of night. It might almost be worth trying to catch an hour's sleep before Fiona got up. Dare he?

Michael Barlow.

The name repeated itself in his mind and instead of going back to bed he began to think about Michael.

***

Rob Moore hadn't known Michael Barlow for long. He had been married to Kate for quite a while before he'd loomed on Rob's horizon. His finger of memory flicked and sorted through the file until he came to the first occasion on which they had met.

It was a party.

A wild party.

In the Moore diary, they were the only kind. The curtain of mist lifted. Yes it was a party—or was it a wake—to celebrate Rob's twenty-fifth wedding anniversary. Twenty five blissful years—and then he had married Fiona. The old joke had a dark reality for him. Fiona... how she had changed over the years. My God, how the bitch had changed. But then so had he. Who was it, he thought, that had changed the most? Was it just a mutual divergence? No. He knew that however much he had altered—physically, mentally, spiritually, he was still recognisable as his young self—maybe as a somewhat bloated caricature now, but still recognisable. The same could not be said of Fiona. She had frozen with the years: the ice-maiden cometh.

Michael Barlow.

The Party.

Kate had brought him along.

Rob's memory of that party was vague in some respects. Mainly due to the fact that even before the doorbell rang, announcing the first guest, he was well on his determined way to being smashed. He liked the world like that—with all the hard edges softened; inside his alcoholic shell he was immune to the slings and arrows of outrageous bloody fortune. While his legs had still functioned, he'd done his dutiful circulation, accepted the congratulatory slaps on the back, the wink-wink nudge-nudge salacious jokes and the badly disguised looks of sympathy; and then as he'd felt himself weaken, he had slumped down in a corner next to...

Next to Michael Barlow.

It was the first time he had met the man.

Of course he had heard things about Kate's husband.

Not nice things.

Apparently, he was a bit of bastard. Or even a whole one; a fully rounded arsehole. But here he was apparently inoffensive, sitting quietly nursing a glass of scotch in subdued seclusion. Surely, thought Rob, this fellow is a kindred spirit. After all, what did they say about *him* behind his back? Well, he could guess. And, he reckoned, most of it would be true.

'Hello there. I'm Rob—mine host. We met at the door, remember?' Michael nodded with the ghost of a polite smile.

'Yeah,' continued Rob, 'This my party, my shindig. To celebrate twenty five years of penal servitude.' He rolled the words around in his mouth before letting them go. 'You enjoying yourself?'

Michael looked down into his drink as though searching for an autocue to frame his reply.

'It's very pleasant,' he said at length, the words carrying no conviction.

'You married? Oh, of course you are. Kate. A lovely lady.'

'Indeed.'

'You're a lucky man.'

Michael shot him a curious look. To this day, Rob could not fathom the import behind that look. He only knew it chilled him.

'How long have you been married?' he found himself asking. The words tumbled out without involvement of the thought process. He desperately wanted to change the subject, but it seemed his mouth and brain wouldn't let him.

'Kate and I have been married for eight years,' Michael Barlow replied, simply.

'Oh, early days,' the mouth said.

'Early days for what?'

'Ah' Rob grinned a most unconvincing grin. He would have to bluster now. Damn the man. Can't he see I'm drunk? Anyway, any civilised fellow would know what I was talking about, what I was suggesting, and even if they didn't, they would pretend they did. 'Oh... for all sorts,' he said, lightly, one hand spinning in a vague windmill gesture. 'How are you fixed for a drink?' he added quickly.

Michael swilled the remainder of his whisky down and handed the empty glass to Rob.

'I would like another. Thank you.'

So would I, thought Rob. 'So would I.' he said brightly, as he took the glass and attempted to stand up, but remained where he was. He giggled. 'I think the legs have gone. Still, that'll please Fiona.' he laughed loudly, but it was a sad, empty laugh. 'Would you do the honours, old man? Help a paraplegic drunk.'

Michael took the glasses, returning with them replenished some minutes later.

'What are you working on at the moment?' he asked, much to Rob's surprise.

'Ah, I've been commandeered to write for a new bloody soap—soap opera—about a firm of solicitors. It's not Hemingway, not even Jeffrey Archer, but it'll pay the rent and the drinks bill. Once, y'know, once I believed I was a writer... a proper writer. I thought television was just a stepping stone to greater things. Hah! For stepping stone read millstone. What the hell, the monster pays well for pap—so pap is what I write. How about you?'

Michael Barlow raised a quizzical eyebrow.

'What do you do? What line of work are you in?'

As soon as the words fell out of Rob's drunken mouth, that small sober corner of the mind that all inebriated men keep— the one which acts as a conscience, letting them realise the mistakes they are making in their drunkenness, without stopping them doing so, that corner which hangs on to reality while the rest of the brain happily succumbs to alcohol—spoke to Rob. It told him what a prize idiot he was. Talk about tactless. He knew that Michael Barlow had not worked since his accident. He couldn't work. Mentally and physically, his talent had been damaged.

In the icy pause that followed his stupid question, Rob Moore felt himself sober up. The pain of reality began to seep back.

Michael Barlow glanced at him with cool disdain. There was no harshness or cruelty in the glance, but there was behind the words he spoke.

'What do I do?' He repeated Rob's question, speaking quietly and slowly. 'I'm a parasite. I live off my wife. She is my bread and butter and my smoked salmon and champagne.' He grinned the coldest grin Rob had ever seen. It made him flinch.

'Rob, come and see what Rex and Marilyn have brought us.' It was rare that Rob was pleased to see Fiona, but her interruption at this point was a Godsend.

'Yes, all right, darling. Let me just get another drink.' He was now too sober to cope. 'Excuse me,' he said, as he rose to go, but Michael Barlow was staring straight ahead in a fixed stare, his fists clenched tight.

***

David Cole could not sleep either.

But his wakefulness had nothing to do with nightmares. At least not dreaming ones. He was worried about Kate and his future with her; or, to be more accurate, whether he had a future with her.

At first she had accepted the death of her husband calmly, stoically. Or so it seemed to him. It was, he believed, in many ways a blessed release and the sadness she felt at Michael's passing was more to do with the failure of their relationship rather than with his loss. She mourned the death of her love for him and how fear and then hatred had replaced it in a seamless descent of her passions. The wound left by Michael's death had been caused by his living not by his passing.

And then slowly, imperceptibly at first, Kate began to feel different. David could sense the new force settling inside her.

Guilt.

Guilt with insidious fingers was twisting her mind, darkening her perceptions.

My God, thought David, what has she got to be guilty about? Michael had been a demon and had made her life intolerable. But Kate was like that. Her sensitive vulnerability was the good earth in which the guilt flourished. She should have been with him when he died. She should have helped him more after the accident, tried to understand him more, loved him more...

And, David was aware that part of this remorse concerned him also. She should not have started an affair with him. Even from the start of their passionate liaison, she had shown signs of uncertainty—wanting him and disliking herself for wanting him. She had never been fully at ease with their relationship.

David gritted his teeth. But now that Michael was dead all that should be over with. It's supposed to be me that she cares for and yet since Michael died, she has spent more time thinking about him. His memory was eating into her, as though it wished to possess her.

There were certain times of late when she had been unable to make love. She had lain in the midnight gloom, shivering slightly, a fine sheen of perspiration on her brow. 'I'm sorry, David,' she'd said, not looking at him. He had caught that distant gleam in her eye as he'd bent near to comfort her. She was somewhere else. Once when they had been making love, her fingers had clawed his back, drawing blood as she called Michael's name out in a strangled gasp.

David stared down at her now. She was at peace in a dreamless sleep, her hands up to her chin holding the covers in a childlike posture. He had vowed he would leave her, he would search for a less complicated lover... But every time he looked at her, especially when she was like this, her beautiful face in quiet repose, he knew he couldn't. He just wanted to, but couldn't.

He lit a cigarette, although he'd vowed that he'd smoked his last a month ago. Stress. More like frustration, he thought, taking a long satisfying drag. The sensation after a month seemed so new to him. He felt like a novice behind the bike sheds. He coughed a little. The cough gave way to a wry chuckle. Smoking to relieve tension—it was a cliché. One he's used many times in his scripts. Now he was acting out his own clichés.

His mind moved back to Kate. Perhaps one answer would be to get rid of the cottage. He knew she loved it so, but it had been theirs: Kate and Michael's. And it still had the feel of him. He's left a dark stain on the air in each of the rooms.

Without conscious thought, David found himself moving about the cottage, prowling almost. It too was now still and peaceful and somehow oblivious to his presence. Without realising it, he had made his way to Michael's studio. He stood before the door, uncertain... uneasy. Gently, almost sensuously, he touched the door with the flat of his hand. This room... yes, it was from here that the sense of Michael radiated. If it was cleared out, redecorated, perhaps it would exorcise his crippling influence.

The door felt cool to the touch. He pushed it open. The studio beyond was bathed in moonlight, which fell through the large skylight. The moonlight hit the glass and seemed to splinter into fine cream-coloured beams. It gave the room itself the texture of a tired old canvas: a medieval painting that with the years was fading like the ruby lips of the Mona Lisa.

Scattered around the room lay several of Michael's paintings, most of which had been torn and mutilated by the artist's own hand. However, on the easel there stood a self-portrait, still intact and startling in its accuracy. The oils glistened in the moonlight, almost animating those strong angular features. David felt himself drawn to it, captivated by its strength.

This was Michael.

It captured not only the features, but also the essence of the man, with the sad cruelty reflected in those fierce blue eyes. The face, even in repose, David recollected, never seemed at ease. The jaw muscles were tight and the skin by the ears rippled gently as though the teeth were being constantly clenched. Michael Barlow stared out from the canvas at David unflinchingly.

A cloud drifted across the moon, catching it in its grey folds and the face darkened.

David flinched with unease as the room closed in around him and the darkness pressed against his body. In the pin-dropping stillness he could hear breathing. It was his own uneasy exhalation.

Suddenly, there came a sharp click behind him. He turned quickly. The door had swung shut. Odd. There was no wind.

He moved to go, although strangely part of him wanted to stay, to stay here in this moonlit half-world amid these mutilated images of reality.

And so for a moment he was held, like a painting himself. Still and indecisive. And then he began to feel cold. A fierce chill entered his body and shook him into movement. He reached the door and shivered involuntarily as he turned the handle. It was icy cold to his touch—the sort of cold that burns. He pulled his hand away, his body shaking uncontrollably. All at once, he felt a strange disquiet—irrationally unnerved in this silent room where a dead man seemed to keep watch. He grasped the handle again and, ignoring the rasping chill to his fingers, began to turn it. Somehow, instinctively he knew it wouldn't turn. He knew it would stick. He gripped it harder, the cold burning his hand.

It would not budge.

He was too rational a man to be frightened, but his sense of unease was growing. There was no reason for the handle to stick. There was no reason for the door to have closed. There was no reason...

Almost like a searchlight being switched on, the moonlight fell into the room once more, dusting it with its frosty light. David turned back instinctively to look at the portrait. This time the pale beams missed the face and it glowered at him there in the shadow.

Or did it?

Was he seeing things?

He took a step nearer to the painting, his eyes concentrating in the gloom, beads of cold sweat dappling his forehead. He must be mistaken—it was a trick of the light. If not... the alternative explanation... well there wasn't an alternative explanation, there was only insanity.

He was rooted to the spot by what he saw or by what he thought he saw in that shadowed room with the stiletto of fear slowly piercing his flesh. It was the face of Michael Barlow staring out from the canvas, the face which now seemed to have the smooth texture of skin. The features had changed. Now they were relaxed and playing about those thin cruel lips was a mocking grin.

David gave a gasp of revulsion and thrust out his hand to push the easel away. It fell with an echoing crash which thundered in his ears. In panic, with a desperate need to escape from the room, he turned back to the door and saw with a mixture of relief and fear that it was now slightly ajar.

***

The Headmaster sipped his coffee and glanced over at Anderton.

'It's fate, Doctor. Unknown forces seem to have taken this business out of our hands.'

'I don't believe in fate,' came the terse reply.

The Head allowed himself an indulgent smile. 'Neither do I. But I do believe in common sense. According to you the boy is fine and can move back to his dormitory by Monday. That is correct?'

Anderton nodded.

'Good. Now we tried to raise the mother last night to no avail. She's an actress, you know.' There was disdain in his voice and the sentence reverberated with implications. 'What is the point of alarming her now that it's all over?'

If it is all over, thought Anderton.

'She's much better left in the dark,' affirmed the Head.

He spoke with such amiable reasonableness and yet Anderton knew that all his considered justifications had nothing to do with the real reason he didn't want Timothy Barlow's mother informed about the 'unusual incident' as he referred to it. He was thinking of the school's reputation. If any hint that there was a pupil with a mystery illness at St Austell's was breathed abroad, it would not be long before the rich parents began to think twice about dumping their offspring at the school. When it all came down to it, it was a matter of money.

So it was with Anderton, he had to admit. If he felt so strongly about the matter, he should tell the Head to get lost and inform the mother himself and to Hell with his contract with the school. But there were financial considerations to be taken into account.

There was the new conservatory his wife had set her heart on. He was slightly disgusted with himself, nonetheless.

'...I'm sure you see the sense of my decision.'

Anderton nodded like a sheep.

'Good. Now, then, how about a little drop of something in your coffee to set you up for the day?'

***

'You OK this morning?'

It was Kate who asked David as they sat at the breakfast table, the warm autumn sunshine flooding in through the window.

'Sort of.'

Kate raised an eyebrow.

David munched his toast, ignoring this invitation to explain himself.

She reached across the table and placed her hand on his. 'I'm sorry, David. I've been a real pain recently haven't? I don't know how you put up with me.'

Because I want you, thought David. Roll telecine of thrashing bodies and delicious moments of interlocking thighs. He said nothing. His silence was more than diplomatic. He reasoned that it would draw Kate on further.

'There's something inside of me that blames me for Michael's death—well, not his death exactly, but his destruction. Oh, I know that sounds melodramatic but it's true. He was gradually destroyed.' Her eyes moistened as she shook her head sadly. 'You see, I can't forget that I loved him once. That thought haunts me. Oh, as you know, I didn't love him at the end, but perhaps I should have done. For better or worse, y'know' She struggled with a fleeting wry grin, but it had vanished by the time she added: 'These thoughts won't leave me. I feel so... responsible.'

David ached to respond to these statements. He could have counteracted her strange obsession with a thousand arguments, but he didn't try. He wanted her to do all the talking. He wanted to hear it all. His comments would only form barriers, stop the flow. This was Kate's release—therapy if you like. She hadn't talked so freely before and he wanted it all to come out, to let the matter seep from the wound.

'When I met you, when I slept with you, I did so because I was in need of comfort. Oh, of course I found you attractive, attentive and all that, but it wasn't loving or sex I was in need of—it was comfort.'

She fiddled with her teaspoon.

'Michael was being particularly beastly at that time. His work wasn't going well and mine was. He called himself a 'kept man'.' She broke off and this time managed to smile broadly. 'But, of course, you know all this. It's ancient history. I'm talking to you as if you were a stranger.' The smile faded. 'Not a stranger, of course but... someone who just doesn't know fully how I feel inside.' She gave a bitter laugh. 'I'm not sure I know myself. Oh... what the hell am I trying to say?'

David left the question unanswered.

'I don't know,' she continued after a pause, shaking her head and staring out of the window, the light brushing her delicate features. 'I just want you to know that I love you, David. I didn't intend to at first but it sort of happened and the mixed up jumble in here,' she touched her brow, 'is of my own making. It's got nothing to do with my feelings for you.'

'I woke up last night and you weren't there beside me. I just felt awful... so alone. I almost panicked. It was like the time when I was a little girl and my father had taken me to the park. I went to feed the ducks. I became engrossed in following some baby ducks around the pond with my bread crumbs, and when I turned round my father wasn't there. I was terrified and began shaking with fear. In my panic I thought I'd lost him for ever. Of course, he was on the other side of the pond keeping an eye on me, but I didn't know that. I felt so isolated. Living with Michael made me feel like that in the end: alone and lost. I don't want that to happen again. Oh, God, all this must sound absolute gibberish.'

David permitted himself a shake of the head. This was better than he had anticipated.

'Last night, I reached a sort of crisis, David. I have been dwelling on Michael's death so much that I thought I heard his voice; I thought I heard him call out to me. Not only that... but I actually thought I saw him—out in the garden. Now I know you must think I'm crazy.'

David's mind shot back to the moment he had arrived at the cottage the previous evening and how he'd seen what he first imagined were two figures on the lawn. Suddenly his mouth went very dry.

'As I lay in the dark last night,' she continued, 'I realised that if I'm not careful, I'll be heading for a complete crack-up, so I gave myself a good talking to.' Her eyes brightened as she gazed directly at David. 'This is day one of the new me. Well, not completely new, but I'm determined to put all the sadness of Michael and the mess of our marriage behind me. I've forced myself to realise that I can't change the past, and as long as I think I can, it will haunt me—destroy me. But I can influence the future. It won't be easy and I don't expect to do it overnight, but will you stay and help me?'

For an icy split-second David had the urge to say: 'The hell I will.' But the moment passed swiftly. He squeezed her hand. 'Of course,' he said softly.

'Thank you,' Kate leaned over the table to kiss him, sending her cup and saucer crashing to the floor.

She grinned. 'Passion with you is always noisy.'

'Let's go to the bedroom; it's much quieter there.' he said.

***

Morning had also found its way into the studio. Michael's portrait shimmered in the bright sunlight—the pale blue eyes stared out fiercely with a malevolent glare.

FOUR

Monday morning. But only just. The big hand had not yet strayed in the darkness to one on the clock. All were sleeping. Kate and David coitally entwined after a renaissance weekend of walks, wine and loving. Timothy, back in his own bed, slumbered deep. But Rob Moore was once more in the realms of dark dreams.

He found himself walking in a dim forest whose trees were tall, straight and strangely smooth like overgrown pencils. They grew close together in a tightly packed formation. In fact, as he made his way through the gloomy forest, guided only by the thin shafts of daylight which fought their way through the thick spread of interlacing leafy branches high above his head, the trees seemed to be closing in on him. Imperceptibly, the gaps between the trunks were diminishing. And yet his feet propelled him on. Deeper into the forest.

Now, in order to progress further, he had to brush against the sides of the trees, his naked arms scraping against the bark. Their touch was clammy and sticky, like no trees he knew. While trying to contain the sense of panic growing in his stomach, he continued to press forward through the ever narrowing gaps.

Soon he was having to squeeze his way between the trunks, the sticky barks leaving dark traces of a greasy jelly-like substance on his flesh. It was ice-cold and it stank. The stuff filled him with revulsion, his stomach heaving with the smell of it, but he couldn't turn back now and he certainly couldn't stay where he was—he felt sure that if he did, he would be crushed by the trees. How he knew this, he couldn't comprehend. But he knew it.

It became a real struggle to force his way through them, pressing his body against the sides, his gorge rising as the foul jelly smeared his face. The trunks of these trees didn't feel like wood at all. They had a different texture somehow—soft and pliable. They felt like... they felt like... flesh!

The roots were now intertwining with each other like the tendrils of some obscene sea creature, further hindering his progress as he kept catching his foot in their spiny network. He stumbled, his face scraping against one of the trunks and he gave out a yell of disgust as some of the jelly substance brushed his lips. He spat furiously to rid himself of the obnoxious stuff. He knew these damned trees wanted him and he realised that it would not be long before he would be crushed by them—crushed and then absorbed through the sticky bark.

He would feed them!

He felt the scream that had been welling up inside him about to burst from his lips when quite suddenly, he squeezed his way out into a clearing.

He was free.

It was as though he had passed through an invisible barrier that was holding the trees back. They ringed the clearing in a perfect circle, standing trunk by trunk as though on guard.

With a frantic flapping of his hands, he scraped and pulled at the vile jelly which still stuck to him, the stuff stubbornly clinging to his fingers. Eventually, rubbing his hands in the grass at his feet, he rid himself of the worst of it and it was then that he saw the cottage. There it was, standing in the forest clearing. Hansel and Gretel eat your heart out. This dream, he thought, must have been concocted by the Brothers Grimm.

His heart lightened as he surveyed the fairy tale cottage. All was still and silent. The door was open and there was a large welcome mat placed on the threshold. The cottage seemed to beckon to him—inviting him to enter.

Rob moved forward down the path, beginning to smile. He was enjoying this part of the dream. He no longer felt threatened or in danger. However, as he neared the front door of the cottage, something caused him to falter, something which at first was intangible, something faint on the air. It was not distinct enough to be definable, but as he took a few more uncertain steps, the sense of it assailed his nostrils and almost overpowered him. From the open door of the cottage came the foulest odour he had ever encountered. The power of it made him retch. Then he recognised it; it was simply the virulent smell of rot and decay. As he fell back from the doorway, he looked up, re-examining the front of the cottage. Then he froze in terror. It was as though a veil had been lifted or one of those gauze back-drops used in stage shows to reveal the hidden scene behind. Now he saw clearly what he at first he thought had been a cottage.

It wasn't a cottage at all.

What disordered short-circuit of his brain had convinced him that it was a cottage? That was of no consequence now. With growing horror, he saw what the thing really was. With smooth walls of skin and black vacant eye sockets as windows, it was a face—a huge, almost human face. And the aperture he had thought was a doorway was its gaping maw.

Good God, it was a face. The face of a rotting corpse.

That face.

Saliva now drooled from its mouth while billows of fetid breath issued forth from the darkness beyond, rolling in sickening waves over Rob. As he stood, frozen with fear, on the threshold of this monstrous thing, he was suddenly thrown off balance by a sharp movement of the ground beneath him and then he felt himself lifted up in the air. As he struggled to keep his equilibrium, he realised with a chilling comprehension that the mat on which he was standing was no mat at all, but the slimy tongue of the monster mouth which was now carrying him into that dark, gaping cavern. He was about to be devoured. As the warm, clammy darkness engulfed him, he threw back his head and screamed.

With a violent jolt forward he sat up in bed. He was ice-cold and drenched in sweat. He did not move for some time, listening to his own thundering heartbeat slowly lessen and feeling his body gradually unclench itself. Everything was still. Fiona slept peacefully at his side, stiff as a corpse. His scream had not penetrated her unconsciousness, although it had been loud enough to wake the dead.

He ran his hand across his wet brow wiping the perspiration away.

Then he heard the laugh.

It wasn't loud. But it was there in the room, somewhere in the shadows—deep and mocking.

What now? thought Rob, What the hell now?

***

Arthur Crabtree slept soundly in his bed. He slept on his back, his mouth open and his cheeks slightly bloated, looking like a blind fish out of water.

His glasses, teeth and toupee rested on the bedside table. All was at peace with Arthur Crabtree. But unbeknownst to him, even in his calm, untroubled slumber, forces were at work on his mind.

***

Out of the shadows at the end of the bed, Rob discerned one more substantial than the rest.

It moved slightly.

Nearer.

The laugh came again, gentle but sinister and cruel. It emanated from this patch of gloom, there could be no doubt about it. This shadow... which Rob knew was no shadow at all. It was something more... real. As it moved again, it looked like a man or rather the shape of a man.

Now he could hear it breathing—a forced stertorous breathing like the painful gasps of an asthmatic... or a dying man. And he could smell it. His body grew rigid again as he recognised that sickly odour that came to him from the darkness at the end of the bed: the smell of his dream had followed him into reality.

The shadow moved again, this time catching a beam of moonlight which filtered through the net curtain. It gave just enough light for Rob to see the face. This time there was no surprise. However irrational the whole thing was, he knew it had to be him. In the creamy light that horrendous visage leered at him with grinning mouth and eyeless sockets.

He grabbed Fiona's arm. He wanted her to see him, too. He wanted someone else to share his madness. He tried to shake her into wakefulness, but she remained immobile. He shook her again, hard this time, and called her name out loudly, but she did not move.

'Fiona, for fuck's sake,' he cried in wild desperation, dragging his wife over on to her back and pulling her up into a half-sitting position. His heart nearly ceased to function altogether at the sight that now met his eyes. Fiona lay slumped against the pillow, her mouth frozen in a twisted grimace. Her eyes were open, but with only the whites visible. But the thing that really shocked him, held him in paralysed thrall, was the sight of the black-handled knife which had been plunged into her left breast, and the dark pool of semi-congealed blood which was forming an obscene pattern around the hilt.

Once again he screamed. And once again with a violent jolt forward, he sat up in bed drenched in sweat.

***

Dawn came.

Arthur Crabtree woke, knowing this was the day for the real contact. He had been troubled for some days by the messages and he knew he would have to respond soon if only for his own peace of mind. But as he busied himself with dressing, he realised these vague feelings had now become a compulsion. The forces within him left him in no doubt.

It must be today.

What he did not realise as he straightened his toupee in the bathroom mirror and examined his tired, grey face was that this dull, autumnal day was to be his last.

***

With a hard, unwavering stare, Nelson Parker, Head of Popular Drama at Paragon Productions, eyed his writing team of Vernon and Sons seated around the highly polished table.

There were four writers in the room, two of whom were David Cole and Rob Moore. They had only exchanged the briefest of greetings that morning. David had been late in arriving and Rob, pale and drawn, seemed tired and preoccupied with his own thoughts. He now sat doodling on his pad, his mind miles away. David naturally assumed that he was concerned about the nature of this special script panel meeting.

'I will not beat about the bush, gentlemen,' said Parker slowly, removing his spectacles and placing them on the polished surface of the table where they mirrored another pair. 'At present Vernon and Sons is in dire trouble. The episodes of the last month were, for want of a better word, crap. Crap with a capital K!' After allowing a brief pause for his considered opinion to have its calculated effect, he leaned forward in a dramatic pose of earnestness and confidentiality. 'You have been far too complacent of late about what we can serve up to the viewer. We are in a very competitive field: the TV screens in this country are awash with soap. If we intend to keep on top, we're going to have to come up with better material than the garbage we've been doling out recently. We are a joke on social media and the viewing figures are plummeting. Quite honestly, it is voiced abroad that it is already too late to save the show... that it's had its day and it's time it was put to rest with a swift and decent funeral. The knacker's yard awaits.' Parker paused and allowed himself a grim smile.

Ben Hughes, the youngest of the writers, opened his mouth to comment, but the gimlet eyes of Nelson Parker froze him before he could speak.

'To put it precisely, gentlemen.' he continued, 'we have three months in which to improve upon these figures or V and S is for the jolly old chop.'

No one spoke, but the atmosphere in the room had changed into one of unsettled gloom. 'Three months,' Parker repeated for emphasis. 'And I had to fight the powers that be bloody hard for that.'

David knew, of old, that a string of rhetorical questions would be trotted out like various tired exhibits at a murder trial to be considered silently before Parker was really ready for discussion. David had not needed Parker to tell him that Vernon and Sons was dying a slow death in front of a diminishing audience. He already knew. The storylines and the performances had been forming a solid mediocre rut for some months now. Most of his own ideas and suggestions had been thrown out by the others on the script panel and by Rob Moore in particular as being too outré or too daring. Rob, as script-co-ordinator, had the final say and he wasn't in the business of taking risks. It was too cosy a number to let David's 'way out' ideas rock his own little boat. David, rather than fight this opposition, had accepted these decisions and meekly gone along with the predictable plotlines that were agreed upon; he had grown tired of the show and was already looking for fresh pastures.

'Well, you are the bright boys,' said Parker with a tired smirk, throwing his arms out to them in a half-hearted gesture. 'If anyone can save the show, you are the ones who can do it. You are the ones who have to do it. So, gentlemen, I'd like to hear your ideas.'

He put his spectacles back on, sat back and glared at them. Ben Hughes made to offer something, but was again silenced by Parker's stare. He must be a distant relation of Medusa, mused David.

'Before you start, I would say this: I do not want to fall back on the old save-the-soap chestnuts of a wedding, a surprise affair or even a sudden death—no Grace Archers need apply.'

David cast a smiling glance at Rob, wondering if he had been serious last Friday about 'killing' Vera Cooper, but Rob did not respond. He didn't look as though he had been listening; his tired eyes were fixed on the middle distance in glazed stare.

'So, gentlemen, the ball is firmly in your court,' Parker announced with a certain finality.

There was a brief pause, everyone waiting to see if he had really finished at last, and then:

'What about some new characters?' The question was posed by Peter Thornton, a wiry Geordie who had joined the writing team nine months before after years in radio drama.

Predictably, David thought, his scripts were too wordy and often too good for the average soap viewer.

'Well, it's possible, depending on budget. Have you anything in mind?' Parker did not seem impressed.

'Not yet,' Thornton replied hesitantly, 'but it's worth thinking about.'

'Of course,' said Parker smoothly, 'any new characters would have to be exceedingly dramatic and spellbinding if they are to establish themselves and up the ratings in three months.'

There was a pause with much nodding of heads and then David leaned forward to speak. Despite the rejection of some of his recent storylines, he was respected by the other writers and by Nelson Parker in particular, who privately considered that he was wasting his time writing the Vernon pap and was worthy of better things, so when David offered an idea in his slow and thoughtful way, he was listened to.

'Why don't we,' he said, 'bring someone back from the dead?'

***

Kate was reading a script when her mobile beeped. It was for a television thriller. She had rejected it once, thinking it trite and too violent for her tastes, but on reflection she now thought it might be a good idea to accept the part. There was no better way of putting the past behind you than by plunging back into work. It would be good to act again, to play at being someone else. This, Kate admitted to herself, was when she was at her happiest. It would also take her away from the cottage and thoughts of Michael. The place encouraged her to brood and to surrender to those awful thoughts of guilt. A hectic television studio would soon shake those from her mind.

Re-reading the script, she quickly became engrossed in the storyline and found to her surprise that she was really enjoying it. So involved was she in it that when the telephone rang and interrupted her reading, breaking the peace of the cottage, she gave a little start as it dragged her sharply back into the real world.

The voice at the other end was unknown to her. It was flat and strangely distant.

'Mrs Barlow?'

She flinched at the use of her married name.

'My name is Crabtree. You don't know me, Mrs Barlow, but it is important that I see you today.'

'What about?'

'I can't really discuss it over the telephone, Mrs Barlow.'

For a fleeting moment Kate thought that this Crabtree may be some kind of cranky fan who had seen her on television and had tracked her down to her home address, just so he could meet her. She was just about to put end the call when he continued.

'I know you must think this is strange, Mrs Barlow, but I assure you that it is absolutely vital that we meet today.' And then he added, almost as an afterthought: 'You see, I have a message from your husband.'

***

'Why don't we bring someone back from the dead?' said David.

There was a moment's pause and then several spoke at once. Rob Moore, who up to this point had seemed detached and preoccupied, turned to David in wide-eyed astonishment. He said nothing but his pale, tired features and shaking hands showed that in some strange way he was perturbed by what David had said.

'Look,' said Nelson Parker, holding his hands up for silence, 'you'd better come clean, David, and explain exactly what you mean.'

'I'd like to resurrect a character,' he said, simply.

'Who?' asked Peter Thornton.

'Margo's husband.'

'John Doyle?'

'Yes.'

'But he's dead,' snapped Ben Hughes. 'You can't bring a dead man back... except as a ghost. You're not suggesting we turn Vernon and Sons into a ghost show are you?'

David gave a wry grin. 'Well, it's an idea.' His grin broadened. 'No, of course I don't mean that. Remember John Doyle was only presumed dead.'

'He died in a plane crash—that's a fairly strong presumption,' Peter Thornton observed dryly.

'Well, the plane crashed and there were no survivors, yes; but Doyle's body was never recovered. Now what if...' he paused here for dramatic effect and to ensure he had their full attention... 'what if he was never on the plane in the first place?'

'What?' Alan Hughes frowned.

David explained. 'Doyle left his wife because he'd had enough of her and the business. As the story went, he packed his bags and flew to South America. En route the plane was struck by lightning and crashed in the sea. End of Doyle—end of storyline. Now at present, Margo is heavily involved with Richard Vernon, the firm's eligible bachelor. What if we make her pregnant and then bring John Doyle back?'

David paused again, but no one spoke. Each was weighing up the feasibility and potential of the idea. All, that is, except for Rob Moore who seemed to have retreated into his own thoughts once more.

'You see,' David explained further, 'Doyle never caught the flight to South America in the first place. He had second thoughts and so he just went away—somewhere—to sort himself out. Now he's done that, he returns to the fold. Imagine the juicy complications: Margo is still legally married to Doyle, but pregnant to another man who was Doyle's superior in the firm. What's Margo going to do? Which way will she jump? Loads of speculation in the press as to the outcome. Real intrigue for the viewers. It will split them into two camps.' He opened his hands palms upwards and glanced around at his colleagues as if to say: 'Howzat?'

'I like it,' said Nelson Parker, smiling and nodding decisively. This was more than his opinion, it was his seal of approval—an assurance of what would happen.

'Yes,' said Ben Hughes, who was learning, 'it's good. Let's do it.'

***

It was hot and stuffy in Crabtree's ancient Punto. Already the sweat was forming under his toupee and trickling down his forehead. He glanced at himself in the driving mirror. What he saw he didn't like. The puffy, blotched face, now damp with sweat, gazed back at him with a stoical sadness. He had the sensitivity to see himself as others did: a fat unpleasant-looking man in cheap clothing. I'm not really like that on the inside, he constantly wanted to tell people, but the unpleasant fleshy trappings all too clearly delineated the man.

As he grew older it had become a real effort on his part to crush these feelings of self-pity. While his body decayed, and the face became etched with further wrinkles and blotches, any hope of self-improvement faded and these dark moods grew more frequent and more immutable.

The car jerked up at a set of traffic lights. A light-coloured Mini drew alongside him. He cast a glance across and saw its occupants were two girls dressed in the bright citrus colours of the young. By some sort of reflex action, they reciprocated the glance and then turning away resumed their animated conversation.

What had they thought of him? Ugly, stupid man. Ugh! Probably, if they'd thought anything at all. The lights changed and Crabtree chugged away in the wake of their roaring exhaust. He might be all those unpleasant things that people thought of him—those that judged by appearance only. But there was more to Arthur Crabtree than met the casual eyes. He had a special gift. A Special Gift. And this gave him Power.

A Special Gift.

He could contact the Dead.

He had only been a child of nine when he first became aware of this—when he had his first other-world experience. It was then that he had seen his dead mother wandering in the tiny garden of their home looking at her beloved roses. She had been no transparent spectre of the story books, but a real-life figure. She had been very real.

That moment had remained vivid and fresh in his memory; he could recall it with great clarity in an instant. His mother had lifted her head from inhaling the scent of a large yellow rose and turned to him, smiling. Her features were serene, and bore no trace of her final, painful illness. 'Hello, Arthur,' she said, her voice clear and strong carried like the scent of the roses on the sultry, summer breeze. Young Arthur had felt no fear at this unexpected appearance of his mother, who had been quite dead for a year. He was neither perturbed nor worried. On the contrary he had felt warm, relaxed... uplifted... and Special.

'Mam,' he'd said, moving towards her, but stopping in his tracks as she retreated, the serene smile still playing about her lips.

'Tell them all, Arthur, that I'm happy, so very happy,' she said finally, merging into the colourful spread of blooms, until he lost sight of her.

'Tell them I'm happy.' The words and the voice stayed with him to this day. It was only later that he understood why his mother appeared to him and not to his father or his sister Emily. It was because he had the Special Gift.

Of course, he wasn't aware of its potential then. But as he grew up he had more other-world experiences and gradually he came to realise that he had the Power. Not only that, but he learned to control it, to use it for his own purpose.

And so the people began coming to him: the grieving, the curious, the emotionally crippled and the cranks. They came and they paid. Paid for his Special Gift.

His powers were strong then and with recklessness and inexperience of youth he used it carelessly—as a means to an end: to obtain women. He loved women—not just with normal appetite of a man. He loved the whole idea of a woman. He loved their flesh, so smooth and fine, so unlike his own rough and blotched skin; he ached to touch and caress it, to run his fingers along it. Sex to him was only a by-product of close body contact, when the feel and smell of a woman would overpower his senses. He would sink and drown happily in the essence of womanhood.

He realised now that he had squandered his Special Gift in satisfying these carnal desires. They had drained him in some way. The sensations he derived from his contact with women, most of them bought and paid for, were transient and as he decayed into middle-age, he found that his Special Gift was similarly transient: his powers waned and then faded away. There had always been a little trickery in his seances—for theatrical effect, because it was what the punters expected and it gave them a feeling that they were getting value for money— but the contact with those on the Other Side had been genuine and potent. Then, gradually, as the real contact began to dry up, Crabtree found himself increasingly having to fake the other-world messages.

Now they were all fake.

He had resigned himself to living the rest of his life as a fraud, a performer of shoddy miracles, when suddenly, without warning, the sensations he had experienced in his youth had returned, more vibrant and stronger than ever. The blinding headaches, the urgent and insistent calling in his brain were there again. But this time there was as difference. This time there was just one voice.

One strident, obsessed voice.

***

'A word, David.'

David Cole turned and found Rob Moore bearing down on him, his pale, haunted face lacking any traces of the sardonic humour that was usually a permanent feature.

'Yes, sure. Down in the bar?'

Rob shook his head. 'Too public. Let's go back to my office. I've got some booze in there'.

David shrugged his shoulders. 'OK'.

He followed Rob down the softly lighted womb-like corridors of Paragon Productions to his office. The script conference was over and the extended lunch hour had begun. Usually Rob was first in the bar and the last to leave it, eschewing food in favour of his beloved spirits. Usually. But today was different.

Once inside his office, Rob poured David and himself a generous measure of Laphroaig and then collapsed in a chair. David expected the conversation to centre on the new plot developments in Vernon and Sons and whether the programme would sink or swim. He was surprised when, after a pause, Rob asked: 'How's Kate?'

'Kate? She's... fine.'

'Is she still... is she getting over... y'know?'

'The death of her husband,' David said coldly, perhaps more coldly than he meant to, but the oblique reference to Michael, the apparently ubiquitous bloody Michael, really irritated him. And what was Rob's concern here? He was far too tense for it to be a polite enquiry and surely it wasn't simple curiosity that prompted him to ask about Kate?

Rob nodded. 'Yes, yes. The death of... Michael.' He paused again and took a large gulp of whisky. David looked at his trembling hands, the dark circles around his eyes and his grey complexion with unease.

'Are you all right, Rob?' You seem a bit tense.'

 Rob forced his mouth into a smile. 'Sure,' he said with some irritation. 'I've just had a couple of sleepless nights, that's all. So how is Kate?' The question was unnaturally brusque.

'Kate's fine. It's difficult to appreciate the situation from her viewpoint, but I reckon she's getting her act together now.'

'Michael doesn't bother her anymore?'

'Bother?' David frowned. It was a strange word to use.

Rob drained his glass. 'She's not bothered by thoughts of Michael?' he added, hoping to clarify the point without being too obvious.

'From time to time. I guess, that's natural. She is a sensitive woman and you can't wipe the memory clean just because a person is dead. Especially a person like Michael.'

'What about you, David? How do you feel about him?'

'What is all this? What on earth are you getting at?' David felt his anger, his irrational anger, rising again and he found it difficult to hold it in check.

Rob poured himself another drink and looked at David apprehensively. 'Getting at? I'm not getting at anything,' he said somewhat defensively, softening his approach. 'I'm just concerned. Old friends and all that.' He tried to smile but the lips couldn't quite make it. 'He was a powerful personality, Michael. Not an easy chap to forget.'

'You didn't know him all that well, did you?'

This time the grin worked and it was unpleasant to see. The face and eyes were frozen in some kind of fear, while the lips glided over the teeth into a fixed grimace.

'I knew him better than perhaps you realised.'

'Oh.'

'Yes.'

David said nothing, but looked steadily at Rob knowing that he needed no prompting to say what he wanted to—what, it seemed to David, he had to.

***

Kate regretted having agreed to see Arthur Crabtree even before he arrived at the cottage, but as she ushered in this strange plump man in shabby clothes, she felt sure she had made a mistake. However, here he was and now she would have to go through with the interview.

'Can I get you a cup of tea?' she asked out of natural politeness.

'No thank you, Mrs Barlow. I never take liquids on the day of a seance.'

Kate shivered at the mention of the word.

Crabtree sat primly on the edge of an armchair and seemed to be waiting for Kate to open the conversation—which, after an uneasy pause, she did.

'Look, Mr Crabtree, I have little time to spare, so would you mind coming to the point and telling me what all this is about?'

In reply he handed her a grubby little card which read:

ARTHUR CRABTREE
Medium & Clairvoyant

Reasonable Rates

Kate looked at the card and then back at Crabtree with a raised eyebrow.

'I've been getting vibrations, Mrs Barlow. Very strong vibrations... from your husband.'

Kate didn't know whether to laugh or cry. 'Vibrations?' she repeated quietly.

'Yes, you see I'm a sensitive and anyone from the other side—those who have passed through the life-death barrier, who have a strong desire to communicate with the living can find a channel through me. I am their mouthpiece, so to speak.' He paused, placing his hands on his lap and offered her a weak smile. 'Ah, I can see that you are somewhat sceptical, dear lady.' Crabtree reached out and touched Kate's hand. He thrilled to the feel of her smooth, cool flesh. Carefully, she withdrew her hand for she found his touch clammy and unpleasant. As he leaned forward, she had become aware of the smell of the man: a cloying mixture of sweat and the odour of mothballs.

'Surely, it is not unreasonable to be sceptical in the circumstances. What you are telling me...' She was lost for words. All she wanted was for this man to leave, to leave immediately without mentioning Michael again. She found herself digging her nails into the palms creating red half-moons of pain there, for she knew, somehow, that he was telling the truth.

'Perhaps I may be allowed to prove to you in a simple way that I am no charlatan, Mrs Barlow?' It was a rhetorical question and Crabtree continued with hardly a pause. 'You were alone in the hospital when your husband died. Although he'd been in a coma for some days, he regained consciousness briefly before he passed to the other side. I know he managed to say something to you before he went, something which I believe you have never told anyone else.'

Crabtree paused dramatically and Kate found herself numb with anticipation. Her features remained calm but the blood pounded in her head almost blocking out any other sound.

Nevertheless, she did hear Crabtree repeat Michael's final words:

'I will come back to you.'

For a moment Kate thought that she was going to faint. The room began to blur and spin; her brow prickled with perspiration and her stomach contracted in a nauseous spasm.

Crabtree leaned over and touched her again. 'Dear lady, do not distress yourself,' he simpered, the unpleasantness of his tainted breath causing Kate further discomfort. She felt his nearness oppressive and this actually helped her to pull herself together. She stood quickly, brushing past him. This simple positive action of moving was reassuring—a confirmation of normality.

Without a word, she poured herself a drink, ignoring Crabtree and the polite procedure of offering him one. After taking a gulp of the harsh liquid, which seemed to set her throat on fire, she turned round on the little medium.

'What is it exactly that you want?' she asked.

***

Rob Moore stared down at his empty glass.

'I knew Michael Barlow better than you were aware.' He paused as though rewinding the film of memory ready for another showing. 'After our first meeting at our twenty fifth anniversary shindig, he sought me out. I suppose he saw in me something of the frustration and disappointment of his own life.' Rob gave a little laugh. 'I tried to persuade him that he had far more going for him than I ever had. But he had an extra burden to carry, or so he thought: Kate.'

'Kate?' David repeated her name with some surprise.

'Yes, Kate. You see he loved her so much... that kind of passion was far more crippling than his damaged hand. Loved her...' his voice trailed away as his eyes stared into the past.

'Love.' he said at length, rousing himself. 'Love? Nah. It was an obsession. He seemed to think that she cared so little for him that it constantly put him on the rack. He suffered real physical pain. It was all so unnatural. You see, the problem was he needed to possess her... completely. And when he realised he couldn't... well, his 'love'—call it what you will—turned into a destructive force. It wrecked the marriage and in the end, it killed him.'

Rob looked directly at David. 'You didn't know, did you, David, that I was with Michael on the day he died?'

'No,' David replied, his mouth becoming very dry. How much more of this was there? his mind asked, feverishly. How much more that I do not know about that damned man?

'Why have you kept quiet about it? Why have you never told Kate?'

'What would be the point? She's suffered enough. Believe me, what I know will ease no one's pain.' Rob leaned back and grinned, or to be more precise, his lips parted and he showed his teeth. There was no pleasure or humour there. 'I'd been seeing Michael on and off for months. Usually for boozing sessions. Mutual despair drink-ins when we'd try to drown our...'—he paused for a while over the word, pain etching lines on his face—'our shortcomings. Michael knew he was losing Kate to you and he felt helpless.'

Rob suddenly laughed out loud and then strangely, tears came to his eyes. 'Let me tell you,' he said with ice in his voice, 'about that last day...'

FIVE

...that last day.

'It's no good, Michael. I am leaving you. There is no point in going on. We are just bad for each other.' She waved her arms in a frantic, frustrated gesture. 'There's just nothing between us anymore.'

God, she wished he'd say something; but all he did was stare at her, stare at her with those chillingly placid eyes. Now it had come to the moment of telling him, now she had drummed up sufficient courage to face him with it, all she could think of were the clichés she had uttered in countless plays and TV dramas. They sounded so crass and banal, but her own emotions were so inarticulate... so confused... that she could not translate them into meaningful statements. She had never given any thought as to how she would tell him that their marriage was over; what had dominated her thinking had been the problem of when... when could she confront him with this awful denouement. And even now as she sat opposite him at the breakfast table, the words had sprung to her lips without planning. It had all happened as though someone else had decided it should.

From Michael's expression she could read nothing. Had he expected this? Surely he had. Maybe not now at this precise moment, but he must have been aware of its eventual inevitability.

His lack of reaction was daunting. There appeared to be no anger or even dismay mirrored in those placid features. There was nothing to play against. Her emotional torrent seemed foolish in such circumstances. There was only one thing for it: she would have to make an exit. She rose quickly from the table but as she reached the door, she was stopped in her tracks by his voice. It was low and neutral, but commanding and hypnotic.

'Kate.'

There was a chilling, threatening tone in the utterance. She had no choice but to turn around and face him.

He looked at her for some moments without speaking and then he said with deliberate slowness: 'I won't let you go.'

The words were like an ice dagger plunging into her heart, but nevertheless she rallied. 'I'm sorry, Michael. I just can't go on living with you anymore. It's driving me crazy.'

'It's Cole, isn't it?'

Kate hesitated. She was under no illusion that Michael was unaware of her relationship with David, but it had never been mentioned before by either of them.

'No,' she replied truthfully. 'It's not because of David. I don't deny I have affection for him, but I'm not leaving you because of him. I'm leaving you... because of you.'

Michael's expression did not change; only his eyes flickered with fire.

'You are mine, Kate. I will not let you go.'

You are mine—the phrase which he had used all through their days together. It had seemed incurably romantic at first, an endearing affirmation of his love for her, but now she saw it for what it was: the ultimate arrogance of brutal possessiveness. And a threat. Michael's use of it now caused something to snap within Kate. Her temper flared.

'I am not yours. I belong to no one. I am my own person and not something that can be owned like a car or a piece of furniture. God damn you, Michael, can't you see that. You demean me by it. You've smothered me with 'you are mine' till I'm choking on it.'

'You are all I have.'

'How can you say that? You are so wrong. You have a God-given talent which you should use.'

'How can I use it with this?' He held up his damaged hand.

Kate knew she was cruel in what she said next, but it was honest and what she really believed. 'You haven't tried, Michael. You use your injury to support your illusion of failure. You always see yourself as the bloody victim, don't you? Poor Michael, Mr Loser, foiled again. For Christ's sake, life is like that. If you're going to sit back and let fate kick you in the face, it will. You've got to fight back—accept the challenge. You can't use people as crutches.'

She was crying now. Hot tears pricked her eyes and blurred her vision. But they were tears of relief rather than sadness. She had at last said what had been bottled up inside her for so long. Her anger and anguish had given her a voice.

'Kate,' he moved towards her.

'No, don't touch me, Michael. Don't touch me. I don't want you. You have to accept that.'

He flung his chair aside in anger. 'I am your husband.'

'No,' she said softly, wiping the tears away, calm now and no longer afraid of his violent gestures. 'No, you're not. You haven't been for a long time. It is over, Michael.'

She turned and walked from the room leaving him transfixed like a video image held on pause.

The next time she saw him, he was dying.

***

Being Saturday, David was having a lie in. He did his lying-in in style: propped up in bed, coffee at his elbow, cigarette in mouth and an array of newspapers spread around him while Miles Davis performed on the iPod for him. He'd never be able to do this if he were married, he told himself on many a Saturday morning. It was to him like a pornographic selfishness.

He had just finished reading a searing criticism of all soap operas in The Independent—an article which on one hand had angered him, while on the other, he had found himself in sympathy with the views expressed—when his mobile rang.

It was Kate.

'I've left Michael.'

There was a pause. It would be wrong to say that David was shocked. He had known for some time that sooner or later he would receive a call like this; but that did not prevent him from being somewhat startled and a little apprehensive when it came. There was a pause, not just because, unusual for him, he was lost for words, but also because he really wasn't quite sure how he felt. He suddenly found his emotions in limbo.

'Where are you now?' he asked at last.

'I've booked in at the Cumberland for the weekend until I've worked out what to do.'

'Why on earth didn't you come here?'

'Uninvited?' Kate had a way with a line which could make it speak volumes.

'Of course,' David replied, ignoring the implications. 'I would have thought that it was obvious.'

'Maybe, but until the dust settles at least, I'm best away from you. I don't want to drag you into our sordid little drama.'

'Too late, I already have a starring part,' he replied flippantly and then added: 'I'm already involved, Kate.' He was surprised at his own earnestness.

'In a way you are, David, but I haven't left Michael because of you. Please understand that. I've left him because I cannot go on living with him anymore.'

'We can meet, at least?'

'Yes of course.' Her voice softened and lost its cold edge. Thank God, he wasn't going to be difficult.

'Where and when?'

'Here, in the bar... say around one.'

'Fine. Kate... How did he take it?'

She gave a cool, mirthless chuckle which reverberated unpleasantly in David's earpiece.

'Like Michael. That's how he took it. Like Michael.'

'Has he made any threats?'

'Not yet.'

***

Rob Moore was pottering about in his garden—certainly pottering and not gardening—when he heard the full-throated roar of an approaching motorbike. He knew the bike and the rider before they drove into view. The Kawasaki screeched to a halt and Michael, clad in black leathers and helmet looking like some kind of satanic angel, dismounted and came up the path towards him.

'You got time for a talk—and a drink?' Michael spat out the question.

Rob had never seen Michael when he wasn't angry or at least when he was just managing to keep his anger burning on a low light, but today there was something fiercely chilling about the harshness of his speech and the ferocity of his stare.

Rob tried to lighten the mood.

'You know me, I've always time for a drinkie. Being Saturday, Fiona's up town spending my money—no doubt on some glamorous underthings that lead nowhere. Come on in, to the house.'

Michael remained in his leathers as he sprawled with squeaking ease on Rob's couch and downed a generous measure of whisky in one gulp. There was silence for a while and Rob knew it was futile to fill in the gap with small talk. He waited, apprehensively twisting his glass round in his hands watching the ice slowly dissolve as he did so.

'Well, she's gone at last,' Michael said at length.

'Kate?' It was a stupid question. Who else? But it was the only response he could conjure on the spur of the moment.

Michael nodded, his eyes ablaze. 'She has finally had enough of me. Gone. Running off to that Cole bastard, no doubt.'

Rob tried to look sympathetic, but he was by no means surprised. In fact, he had been expecting this turn of events for some time. He knew of David and Kate's affair—they made a good couple—but David was not the reason for Kate leaving. He was sure of that.

He refilled Michael's glass to cover his uncertainty at what to say.

Suddenly, Michael seemed to relax, his body visibly softened and extended itself. The hunched shoulders and tense posture melted while his face almost folded into a smile. He was staring far off—beyond Rob, beyond the walls of the room—far beyond.

'She'll not get away from me, y'know,' he said softly the eyes still lost in this other dimension. 'Oh no. Never. Whether she likes it or not, she's mine, body and soul.' His features remained neutral as he repeated simply: 'She's mine.'

Rob was at an even greater loss for words now and so he quickly poured himself another drink. Turning back, he found Michael studying him, his blue eyes like twin electric drills boring into him. He felt the skin on the back of his neck begin to creep.

'You knew, didn't you? You knew she was seeing David Cole—that she was sleeping with him?' The voice was low, but very vicious. He made the word 'sleeping' sound like some utterly vile pornographic abomination.

Rob did not answer. He found his tongue drying up within his mouth.

'Oh yes, you knew. No doubt you actually helped your friend to commit adultery with my wife.'

Rob knew he was in danger, but he couldn't move, paralysed by those blue eyes and the fierce threat they held. Suddenly with a swift impulsive movement, Michael leapt from his chair and grabbed Rob by the throat, his strong left hand virtually circling Rob's neck, the fingers pressing hard into his flesh. With instinctive panic, Rob tried to move, but Michael held him down with his left arm, pressing him back in the chair.

'You will regret your connivance. You are part of their conspiracy and, trust me, you will pay.' Michael hissed, bringing his face closer to Rob's as he tightened his grip.

Rob was terrified. He felt his body weaken under the pressure, but he had no fight in him to retaliate. As Michael loomed over him, his face was beginning to grow misty, the eyes growing larger, spilling down his cheeks, the whole merging into the blackness which was seeping in around the peripheral areas of Rob's vision. My God, he thought, I'm going to die. I'm going to die! The devil is going to strangle me.

Sweat began to pour down Rob's forehead as he felt his body begin to soften and melt as though all the bones had been removed from his body. He tried desperately to gasp for air but Michael's fingers pressed hard on his windpipe.

And then Michael released him.

Coughing and spluttering, Rob gasped for air. With watering eyes, raw throat and thumping head, he grabbed hold of reality once more. As he sucked in the air in eager gulps, his throat felt as though he had swallowed a broken bottle. Gradually, as his breathing eased and vision cleared, he saw Michael reclining once more on the sofa, his arms casually spread out along the back and a satisfied Cheshire Cat smile on his lips. The bastard had enjoyed half-killing him!

'I think you'd better go,' said Rob hoarsely.

'Certainly,' said Michael, but made no attempt to leave. He remained relaxed and immobile on the sofa.

Rob felt like he was involved in one of his own scripts and he had written himself into a corner. There was nothing either character could say that would resolve the problem. So in the hissing silence, the two men sat quietly, staring at each other, held in a waxwork tableau.

Eventually Michael moved. His actions were easy, all aggression in gesture and expression had gone, but in his fluid movements there was that hint of madness, that obsession which was far more frightening than his anger.

'I won't forget your complicity, Mr Moore... and neither will you.' he said amiably, with a smile. It was only his eyes, dark with menace that held the truth. They burned with a vicious sourness that paralysed Rob again. He sat limply in the chair unable to move, as Michael brushed past him. Reaching the door, Michael turned and flung a final comment at him: 'You will be sorry. Count on it.'

With that he was gone.

But Rob was to see him one more time.

***

A shaft of autumn sunlight filtered through the grimy mullioned window and fell on the worried countenance of Timothy Barlow as he entered the room. His father, who was still dressed in his black motorcycle leathers, turned to greet him.

Michael's sudden and unexpected appearance had caused ripples of consternation in the calm waters of St Austell's private school that Saturday afternoon. It was unheard of for a parent to arrive without an appointment and for him to be dressed as a Hell's Angel further increased the corporate consternation. We do not vet the parents carefully enough, thought Saunders, the house master on duty, as he had spoken to this lout. Unfortunately, it is only their bank balance that concerns the head, not their breeding.

Saunders had been cool and off-hand with this over-bearing leather-clad stranger who had demanded to see his son.

This is most irregular, Mr Barlow. We request that parents inform us of their intended visits in order to make appropriate arrangements in advance.'

'Are you saying that I can't see my own son?' The words were spoken softly but there was an underlying ferocity in the man's voice that unnerved Saunders.

'No, no, of course not, but...'

'Let's leave the buts out, shall we? I'd like to see Timothy... now.' The housemaster withered under Michael's stare and hurried out to fetch the wretched Barlow boy.

'Is there anything wrong, dad?' asked Timothy, shambling forward towards his father, apprehensively.

Michael clasped the boy, pressing him against his body. Timothy felt himself being smothered by the smooth black leather. The strange clammy odour turned his stomach. Unnerved, he struggled free.

'What is it dad? Is mum all right?'

'Oh yes, your mother is absolutely fine.' The sarcasm in his voice was lost on Timothy.

'Why are you here then? Why did you come?'

'To see you, that's all. To see you and say goodbye.'

'Goodbye? What do you mean? Where are you going?'

'Ah, that's a secret.'

'You'll be coming back though, won't you Dad?'

Michael stared ahead of him at the shaft of sunlight still falling through the window, the yellow light rippling with a myriad of dust particles.

'You can bet on it, son. I will be back.'

***

Autumn was on the land. The trees in the garden of the cottage, stunted and gnarled by their countless battles with fierce coastal winds, were almost bare. Only a few leaves, like little burnt rags, clung on tenaciously against the nagging wind, a futile fight against the inevitable. The branches of the hornbeam close by the picture window of the sitting room tapped skeletal fingers on the glass as though it wanted to gain entry. Michael gazed out at the autumn greyness in final despair. His vision was blurred, partly by alcohol, but his thoughts were knife sharp. Life, he concluded, had turned completely sour. But then for him it had never been sweet. He had been born with lead weights in his soul. Kate could have saved him from his own bitterness - but she hadn't. Nevertheless, she had been the one bright, comforting spark in the gloom of his existence.

At the thought of Kate, he trembled with emotion. Passion and fury merged into a searing sensation which shook his frame and thundered in his head. The power of it made him wince. His future, he thought, was like that bleak October sky out there—a grey void, an empty nothingness.

A new thought struck him and caused him to move. He walked purposefully, but with an easy relaxed motion and he found himself almost smiling. At the door of his studio, he hesitated for a moment before entering. This had been his domain. It was here that he had achieved some kind of fulfilment. Had. Past tense. He felt no joy in this room now; now it seemed like some ghastly hall of mirrors. Distorted reflections of life as he once had observed it stared back at him in mute enmity.

He fingered some of the canvases with mistrust. Their surfaces were cool to the touch. Stretching his damaged hand onto the face of one painting, he forced the gnarled fingers apart until they splayed wide. He flinched with the pain of it, but he did not relax his muscles. Now with his hand flat on the canvas, he slowly curled his fingers until the nails found purchase on the paint-roughened surface and then calmly, deliberately he pressed hard until one by one, his nails punctured the surface of the painting.

He gave a grunt of satisfaction.

Then with a sharp pull and tug of his hand, he viciously snatched away a portion of the canvas in his grasp, leaving a jagged aperture at the heart of the picture. As he stood back, his hand throbbing with the strain, he smiled in grim satisfaction at the damage he had caused. It was, for him, a supreme moment of creation.

***

Rob approached the cottage as dusk was seeping into the sky. There were lights on in nearly all the rooms. Michael's Kawasaki was abandoned in the drive, tilted at a drunken angle, but there were no other vehicles there.

All seemed strangely still.

What was he doing here? Rob asked himself. Why was he getting mixed up in other people's lives, other people's problems? Why should he care a toss about Michael? Damn the man, he had nearly strangled me a few hours ago. Rob knew that he couldn't answer these questions logically. Logic and emotions (not to mention drink) are strange bedfellows. It was a strong irrational compulsion that had driven him to seek Michael out. He felt it in his bones that the stupid bastard was about to do something drastic; the clown needed saving from himself.

Rob Moore to the rescue!

The house seemed empty.

He moved from the hall into the kitchen and then into the living room. He hesitated a moment before calling out Michael's name. As he did so, it reverberated in the silence, losing itself somewhere in the recesses of the cottage.

There was no response.

The Studio.

Of course, Rob mused, that's where the bastard will be skulking.

When he reached the landing, he found the door to the studio half open. Entering, Rob gasped at the scene of mutilation that greeted his eyes. Canvasses shredded, torn and slashed lay strewn around the room. Portraits and seascapes now mangled and maimed formed small twisted heaps littering the floor.

Few paintings had escaped the carnage. One that had was propped on the easel, remarkably still upright, standing alone amongst the debris and aloof directly under the skylight. It was a portrait. His portrait. The face of Michael peered out on the scene of destruction with cool disdain. As Rob caught the eyes, he sensed they were focussed on him, accusingly. Their icy stare held him, driving a hole into his mind. Fierce bursts of pain exploded in his head and his limbs stiffened with an irrational fear. He felt revulsion for that painted face that glared at him from the lifeless canvas. He had to get away from those eyes which, like dark pokers, were singeing their way through his flesh. He turned sharply to move away, but his feet were slow to respond and he staggered backwards as they became tangled with a large broken frame. In panic, he lost his balance and fell, cracking his elbow on the floor. He cried out and clamped his eyes shut as fierce pain shot up his arm.

When he opened his eyes again, they were misted with tears caused by the sudden hurt. He wiped them away with his sleeve and as his vision cleared, he looked up to see the portrait of Michael louring over him. His moan of pain gave way to a dry gagging croak of terror as he saw the expression on the painted face of Michael Barlow change. The features subtly shifted in the grey light, eyes twinkling with malicious glee while the mouth formed a tight smile.

Rob fled the room.

Flinging open the landing window, he leaned out and took in large gulps of cold, fresh air. Somewhere out in the growing night, he heard lull of waves beating against the rocks. It was a soothing, restful sound. Slowly he felt a sense of reality return and with it the increased throbbing ache in his arm.

Closing the window, he gave a sardonic grin. His imagination had been working overtime, he reasoned. However, as he cast a furtive glance back towards the studio, he was sure that he did not want to go back in there, imagination or not. What he needed was the bathroom and then he would get the hell out of that damned house. Sod Michael! Sod him to death!

But what Rob Moore did see when he went into the bathroom had nothing to do with his imagination. It was real—horribly real. Michael lay in the bath, his head resting between the taps as though it were jammed there. His eyes were closed but his mouth gaped as though emitting a silent snore. The bath was empty except for two dark pools of blood forming around his limp wrists, each of which was ruptured with a jagged gash, still dripping with the red syrup of life.

A blood-spattered kitchen knife lay in his lap.

On meeting this sight, Rob Moore froze with mind-numbing shock. He just stared in silent horror while the grisly scene carefully and vividly etched itself on his mind for ever.

And then...

And then, like a nightmare, Michael's eyes opened, and his mouth relaxed.

'Hello, Rob,' said the voice from the edge of the grave.

***

Sebastian Riley was losing again. He didn't mind. He just enjoyed the fun of the game. And fun was low on the agenda at St Austell's. As it was in any prison camp, he supposed. Saturday tea-time gave him his best moments of the week. It was the free recreational period with no brutes of masters hanging around, eager to impose extra work on their ill-used charges.

As Sebastian counted out the numbers, he could see Park Lane looming up. Oh, well, he thought, if I'm going to be wiped out what better address than this.

'Mine.' cried Timothy Barlow with avaricious glee. 'That's mine. Oh Sebby, you've had it now. He consulted his property card. 'Park Lane with a hotel—that'll be fifteen hundred, please.' He held out his hand for the money.

'What? Fifteen hundred?'

'C'est ça.'

Sebastian examined his diminished riches. 'I can't pay. Can I owe you?'

'No chance. You'll have to sell something off. What about your stations?'

'Oh, they're my only money makers.'

'I know.' Timothy beamed.

Sebastian knew that he was only delaying his inevitable bankruptcy, but he agreed. After the transaction had been completed, Timothy, with a smirk of satisfaction, took up the shaker for his go and then suddenly, with a sharp intake of breath, he threw it down as though it were on fire. He gave a cry of pain and fell back in his chair, the colour draining from his face and eyes staring wildly about him.

'What is it? What's wrong?' asked Sebastian, not sure whether his friend was being serious or not.

'Pain,' gasped Timothy. 'Awful pain.'

'Where?'

'In my wrists.' Timothy held out his hands as in an act of supplication and Sebastian could see angry red bruises marked across each wrist.

***

'Emergency, which service do you require?'

There was a pause and then a man's voice said, 'There's been a terrible accident. A man has been wounded... badly. His wrists... Needs medical assistance urgently.'

'Where? What address?'

The voice, hesitant and strained, gave the details and then hung up before more information was required.

***

It was nearly midnight when Kate got to the hospital. It had taken the authorities some time to trace her and from what the doctor had said on the telephone, she knew she might well be too late. As she pushed open the swing door and moved out of the cold night air into the hushed and temperate atmosphere of the hospital, she asked herself—too late for what? Too late to be in at the kill? It was certainly too late for anything else.

After the initial shock she received at the news of Michael's suicide attempt, her emotions had gone into a kind of limbo. The thought of Michael dying had an anaesthetising effect on her sensibilities. She really did not know how she felt. If anything, she was angry—but angry about what or with whom she couldn't say.

A sympathetic night sister took her to Michael's room.

'He is unconscious. I'm afraid...' she began.

'Yes, I know,' said Kate quickly, saving the sister the task of telling her that Michael would never regain consciousness again, that there was no hope, and that he would be dead within hours.

She moved to the bed and looked down at the gaunt yellowish face lying on the pillow. In the muted light, his skin seemed to have the texture of wax, like wax fruit—lifelike but not real.

Kate began to cry. She didn't really know why. Was she weeping for Michael, for herself, or for the dream that had died? Here was the man she had once loved and the ache in her heart increased as she knew with a chilling bitterness that despite everything, she could feel no love for him now—not even as he lay dying. That was her tragedy.

'Oh Michael,' she said, almost in a whisper.

At the mention of his name, the pale mask of a face flexed itself slightly: the eyelids twitched and the forehead puckered.

Using it like a magic charm, Kate chanted his name again. This time his eyelids prized themselves open and gradually his bleary eyes focused on her, the pupils dilating into large dark circles. She moved closer and spoke his name for a third time. Recognition sparked in his eyes and almost without moving his lips, he spoke to her, his voice faint and distant.

'Kate. I've been waiting for you to come. I've been hanging on.' There was a long pause and the lids crept down over his eyes but Kate could tell that he hadn't finished, that he had more to say, so she waited quietly. Eventually, he summoned up enough energy to speak again. And for the last time.

Turning his head towards her and almost smiling, he said: 'I will come back to you.'

By the time Dr Muncaster had arrived minutes later, Michael Barlow was dead.

SIX

'Why didn't you say anything about this before?'

Rob shook his head. 'I don't know. I was somehow frightened. When I found Michael in the bath like that... I just phoned for an ambulance without giving my name and then I ran—ran as though my life depended on it.'

'What had you to be afraid of?'

'Guilt, I suppose. My own guilt. In some way I contributed to Michael's death.'

David shook his head sadly. Not you, too, he thought.

'Look, David, please don't tell Kate... or anyone about this, all right?'

David nodded in agreement. Nothing could be gained by that now, not a year after Michael's death. Nothing would be solved by adding further disturbing details of the man's demise. Rob's revelation didn't alter the facts anyway. The bastard was dead and the sooner he was forgotten the better. Now that Kate had finally come to terms with the situation, he had no wish to reopen the wound.

'I won't say a word. But why, after all this time have you felt it necessary to tell me?'

For a fleeting moment the gaunt and haggard features of Rob Moore softened into a little mirthless smile. 'He's been haunting me, David. In my dreams. He won't leave me alone. He wants me. He's come back to take his revenge. Crazy isn't it? A man of my age frightened to go to sleep—but I am. You've no idea... how real the dreams are. Oh, I can guess what you are thinking. It's my own conscience at work—the air drawn dagger of the mind, right?'

David did not reply.

'It's not remorse that keeps me awake; it's fear. I just feel scared. My whole life has lost its balance. My waking moments are like a dream and those damned nightmares are my new reality.'

'Rob, you have got to stop this now before it gets out of hand. No matter how real these dreams seem to you, they are only tricks of your own subconscious. Just dreams. Life is real. Here and now is life. Dreams are only shadows in the imagination. Michael Barlow is dead; he's buried six feet under. He can't come back; it's you that's resurrecting him in your dreams.'

Rob closed his eyes and shook his head vaguely.

'You need a psychiatrist, Rob. He'd straighten you out. Do something soon. Nip this obsession in the bud before it blossoms into something really dangerous. I know a man who's very good. I could arrange an appointment for you.'

Rob stared blankly. David was being very kind—rational. But he just didn't realise. He just didn't know.

'Rob,' David prompted sharply.

'OK, OK. Organise an appointment with your shrink,' Rob replied with a trace of the old sarcasm in his voice.

'Fine, I'll do that today. We'll soon have you sorted out.' He gave his friend a reassuring pat on the arm and smiled. 'Tell me, these dreams—they only started recently?'

'Yes.'

'Why do you think this is? I mean Michael's been dead for nearly a year—why should you start having nightmares about him now?'

'It is a year. One year exactly. One year today. It's Michael's anniversary today.'

***

When Arthur Crabtree returned to his tiny terraced house, Jean Wilson was waiting for him on the doorstep, pale and stick-like. It was she who for the last three years had helped Crabtree with his work. Her only reward for this labour was to spend some time in close proximity of the man who she hoped one day would ask her to marry him. Through her thick pebble lenses

Arthur Crabtree loomed as a graceful saviour, a spiritual hero. He was seen as he himself wanted to be seen. However, Jean held no such attraction. For him she was a scraggy, thin, simpering old maid whose gullibility and vulnerability had been useful to him in his trade, especially since the decline in his natural powers.

'Oh, Arthur, at last,' she smiled at his approach, clutching her handbag in both hands.

He granted her a greeting and strode past her to fit the key in the lock.

'Is there a meeting tonight?' she asked, following him into the dingy hallway that smelt of dampness and stale cooking fat.

'Indeed there is. A very special one.'

'Oh.' A tremor of excitement ran through her. 'In what way 'special', Arthur?'

He turned to her, his face sheened with perspiration, his eyes flickering with mixed emotions. He was half-afraid and half-excited.

'I'm in real contact again,' he said softly. 'Real contact. And I've got to unburden someone. Someone here.' He tapped his forehead. 'In my head. He won't leave me alone. Tonight, the powers willing, I will release him. If I don't, he will drive me mad.'

***

It took David sometime to settle down to work that afternoon. The talk he'd had with Rob had unnerved and depressed him. It wasn't the facts about Michael's death that were disturbing; it was what was happening to Rob. Easy-going laconic Rob. He had disappeared to be replaced by a frightened, nervous replica. It was though Michael had powers beyond his death to screw up other people's lives. It had happened with Kate—thankfully that was over—and now it was Rob.

With chilling clarity, he saw that logically he would be next. Surely he was stronger and far too rational to be influenced by memories of a dead man. It was the mind only that weakened and became susceptible to such fancies. But not with him. He felt no guilt or sorrow for Michael Barlow's death. Good riddance. He was not about to become a member of some guilt-hallucinating coterie.

And then he remembered that night in Michael's studio. And the portrait, Michael's face. A living face.

Suddenly he felt sick.

The internal phone buzzed and half in a dream he picked it up. Nelson Parker's incisive voice reverberated in the plastic earpiece. 'David. I liked what you said this morning about V and S. Creative thinking—a rare commodity in TV at the moment.' He paused for David to respond but he remained silent. 'In connection with that, I'd like you to call in at my office around four this afternoon for a chat. OK?'

'Yes, that'll be fine,' said David flatly.

'Good. See you then.'

The call brought David out of his reverie and he began to draft out the episode in which Margo's husband would return, as it were, from the grave.

***

Jean Wilson drew the curtains in Arthur Crabtree's parlour. It was a dull day and although it was around three in the afternoon it was quite dark.

'I want none of the fake stuff tonight, Jean,' Crabtree said, as he sat hunched up over the meagre fire in the grate. 'Tonight's for real.'

'For real.' There was a thrill of pleasure in Jean's voice as she repeated the words. As long as she had been helping Arthur with his work, she had never witnessed a meeting when he didn't use some of his 'artificial aids' in contacting the other side. Some of them were very spectacular: the cheesecloth ectoplasm and the disembodied head of his familiar (controlled by Jean) had startling effects on his clients who were usually anxious and gullible widows and widowers more than eager to accept the sideshow trappings that accompanied the messages from their loved ones.

'Not even the crystal ball?'

'Not even that.'

Jean came and sat opposite him and touched his hand. 'Will it be safe, Arthur? Will you be safe?'

In the firelight he saw his own distorted image reflected in Jean's pebble lens. 'I don't know. I just don't know...'

***

Just before he left his office for the meeting with Nelson Parker, David rang Mark Salberg, the psychiatrist he had told Rob about and arranged an appointment with him. He then checked his answering machine. There were four messages: two internal calls wanting information; a strange call with thirty seconds of static; and the fourth was a message from Kate.

'Darling, sorry I didn't catch you but I'm just ringing to tell you that I'll be late home tonight. I've been rereading 'The Spider Trap'—you know that spy thriller that I was offered and turned down. Well I've changed my mind. I've decided you were right and it's time I got back into the swing of things. So I'm going to do it. I'm having dinner with the producer tonight to discuss it. OK? Don't wait up for me. Bye.'

She sounded unnaturally cheerful to David. However, despite not being able to see her that evening, he was pleased she was taking positive action about her career at last. Her meeting that night would be really good for her.

***

Dusk came haunting the quadrangles of St Austell's.

Timothy Barlow gazed out from the dimly lighted classroom as Kenworthy, the maths master, droned on. He watched the growing gloom with unease. He had thought about his dad a lot today. It was a year since he'd died. He remembered that and it made him sad, like the coming darkness. Not having a dad was no fun. It made you different from the other boys. Of course, there were others in school whose fathers were dead, one or two, but none whose father had... killed himself. He still found it hard to say that. If only he had died naturally, in an accident or

71

something—but to actually kill yourself—well, it's what mad people do.

He thought his mother might have rung or come down today just to give him a bit of comfort. Of course, she didn't know he hadn't been well and that he'd had a kind of fainting fit. Best not to worry her was what Matron had said. But he wanted to worry her. He needed her for reassurance. He only had her now. But she had been strange since his dad...

He suddenly got an image of his father in his motorcycle leathers on that day a year ago, the last day he had seen him.

'I will be back.' That's what he had said. He hadn't kept his promise.

Yet.

The quadrangles began to merge into the darkness. He didn't like the night. It worried him. Especially today. He had been feeling troubled and strange all day; but he didn't want to mention it—not after his fainting fit. Besides there was no one he could confide in. He knew he had to keep his feelings and secrets to himself. With relief, he returned to his own dormitory. Usually he felt safe here, but this evening was different. His senses were on edge, disturbed, as though something was reaching out of the darkness to touch him.

***

Mist was already shrouding the cottage when Kate set off. She shivered as she fumbled with her car key which somehow refused to fit the slot. It wasn't the October cold that made her shiver: it was nerves. She had been like this ever since Crabtree had left her. One moment she was telling herself that she was ridiculous and stupid agreeing to attend that awful man's seance and the next she was thrilled at the thought of being in contact with Michael again. It would give her the opportunity she had longed for; the chance to ask his forgiveness.

But contact with the dead... that wasn't really possible. Once you were dead you were...

As she started up the car and the yellow fingers of her headlights cut into the darkness, she remembered her experience on Friday night. The mist and the man-shape and Michael's voice. And how had Crabtree known what Michael said to her just before he died.

'I'll be back.' She knew the questions but was too frightened to consider the answers.

Kate tried to console herself that at least one way or other this night would lay the ghost of Michael once and for all. That was how she would view this evening's proceedings: in a positive light. It would also help her to feel less guilty about lying to David where she was going that night. It was with great relief when, on ringing him, she had found that he was out. It was much easier to pour her lie into his answering machine which could not challenge her deceit.

It wasn't long before she was in Brighton, dismal and dead in winter, and then heading for the hinterland of gloomy terraces and crumbling council properties, to the house where she hoped to contact her dead husband.

***

As Arthur Crabtree lay still on his bed, staring at the ceiling, the light from the sodium street light outside threw a shadowed mosaic onto the walls of the darkened room. He breathed shallowly, self-inducing the surface consciousness to leave his body. His mind, however, would not go blank. It retained a nagging image—the face that would not fade.

He had eaten and drunk nothing in preparation for the meeting and now he was feeling tired and weak. He dug deeper into the mind's resources, pushing back the barriers of consciousness.

Gradually the face began to fade; as it did so it grew smaller until eventually it resembled a spot of light in the void of his mind. And then the image of his mother flitted into view. She smiled sweetly at him. It was the same smile she had given him all those years ago when she had appeared to him in the garden when he was nine.

Her smile broadened and twisted. So did the face. It contorted, the flesh rippling and buckling, exploding in pustules. Then his mother's face broke open violently like a mask splitting in two and behind the mask was another. It was that face again – the one that haunted him. And it was grinning.

***

Downstairs in the silence, Jean Wilson prowled, pumping a cushion here, straightening a chair there. She gave the little piano another wipe with the duster, allowing her fingers to run along the keys. Gazing around the gloomy chamber, she gave a satisfied smile. Everything must be just right for tonight.

Tonight was special.

Tonight she was to see her beloved perform a true contact with the other world. There would be no gimmicks, no trickery. This time it was to be the real thing.

***

Kate sat in her car and stared at the front door of Crabtree's terraced house. It looked ordinary, unremarkable, in a row of similar houses. True, it was a depressing street with obvious signs of decay and neglect but nonetheless, it was normal. Was it here that she would really be able to speak to Michael again?

Suddenly she felt very stupid. What would David say if he saw her here, now, playing some farcical spook game with Crabtree who was either some kind of charlatan or crank. He would most likely have her certified. He certainly would drop her like a hot brick. And who could blame him? Who would want to stay around a woman who was trying to pass a message on to her dead husband? This was ridiculous; she must leave before the farce actually began.

Kate put the car into first gear and turned the engine on. Nothing happened; there was no reaction at all. It was lifeless. In some strange way this did not surprise her. She tried again, her mind telling her body to go through the motions, while at the same time knowing that it was useless. The engine did not even turn over.

She glanced at Crabtree's door: number 69. Its green paint was flaking—a nonentity of a door—yet it beckoned. Instinctively she felt drawn to it. Somehow, she knew that she had to enter. It was Fate and who was she to deny Fate?

Suddenly she noticed a dark figure in front of the car. She could see nothing of its features as it stood against the light of the street lamp. With slow deliberation it moved around the side of the car. She heard the passenger door handle turning. She looked across. It was unlocked. She leaned over quickly to press the lock down. But she was too late. The door swung open and chill air swept into the car. The silhouetted figure leaned forward towards Kate, the gaunt features illuminated by the lights from the dashboard.

'Anything wrong?' said a polite, serious voice.

Kate felt a wave of relief. She managed to produce a smile for the policeman. 'Er no. I'm just calling on a friend. Mr Crabtree at number 69.'

'I see. Engine all right? I thought you seemed to be having some trouble.'

'No, no. Everything's fine.' She was lying again and she began to feel nervous.

The policeman's immobile features, ghoulish in the green light of the dashboard, stared back at her in disbelief. She turned the key in the ignition. The engine purred gently.

'Everything's fine.'

'Sorry to have bothered you then.' The figure withdrew.

'Thank you anyway.' she called after him.

'That's all right,' he called back as he closed the passenger door.

She watched as he walked down the street. On reaching the street lamp he turned and glanced back at her. Kate felt guilty of some unknown crime. No, it wasn't unknown. She had lied. She had... Oh, she didn't know what. The whole business was ransacking her mind.

With sharp urgent movements, she left the car, locked it and glancing briefly at the still watching policeman, and made for that green door with the peeling paint.

***

It was dark when Rob Moore left the offices of L.T.V. He had spent most of the afternoon staring at a blank notepad, willing ideas to come to him, trying to block out other thoughts—thoughts that threatened his sanity.

He had failed.

As he made his way to his car, he realised that he couldn't face the prospect of spending an evening at home with Fiona nagging at him. Even the indifferent Fiona had been showing some concern over his behaviour in the last couple of days. The thought of her remorseless interrogation made him shudder.

Some miles from home, he pulled off the road into the car park of the Shoulder of Mutton. He'd spend a few hours here before braving the domestic front. Perhaps a good dose of Dr Johnnie Walker's medicine would cure all his ills.

***

The door was opened by a thin, unhealthy-looking woman in thick glasses who introduced herself as Mr. Crabtree's 'helper'. She offered to take Kate's coat, but Kate resisted. She felt vulnerable as it was and keeping her coat on somehow gave her the feeling of being a little more secure as though, if necessary, she could make a speedy exit without hindrance.

On entering the hall, the stale stench of the house assailed her, and she felt as if she would choke. All self-control seemed to be leaving her as though she had surrendered to some hidden force that had led her into this mad excursion. She dug her nails into the palms of her hands, the sharp pain helping her to keep in touch with reality.

Crabtree's 'helper' showed her into the darkened parlour.

'Please sit yourself at the table. I'll let Mr. Crabtree know you've arrived. He is upstairs at present, preparing himself for tonight's contact.' After these words, the strange-looking woman glided from the room as if she herself was a wraith, from a dark region.

Kate did as she was bidden and sat on the edge of a chair at the round dining table. There was a dusty shade suspended above it casting down a gloomy circle of light on to the surface of the table. This and the meagre fire in the grate were the only forms of illumination in the room. For a fleeting moment, Kate had the illusion that she was on some studio set. The whole thing wasn't real. And neither was she. She was playing a character in some weird melodrama.

Any moment now the props man would appear to sprinkle a little more dust around and stir up the fire into more life.

But he didn't come.

She heard sounds from upstairs. God, what was she doing here? Could she leave now before Crabtree came down? She half-rose from her chair and then the face of Michael flashed into her mind. No, she must stay, stay and settle this once and for all. It had to be faced.

'Good Evening, Mrs Barlow. I'm so glad you have come to the meeting.' Crabtree came across and took her hand in his clammy grasp. 'It is a meeting of the two sides: the living and the spirit world. There will be no others present except ourselves and Miss Wilson who will be assisting.' He smiled an oily smile. 'Are you ready, my dear? You know your friend on the other side is most anxious to speak with you. Your friend, Michael.'

'My husband.'

'Quite so. Are you quite prepared?'

How can I answer such a question sensibly? Kate thought. Am I ready to speak to my dead husband? How can anybody be ready for such a thing?

'You will not disappoint him?' asked Crabtree with a trace of concern in his voice.

'No, no,' Kate replied quickly. 'Please... go ahead.'

Let's get it over with, her mind screamed.

'Excellent. That is brave of you, my dear. I realise how stressful all this is, but be reassured you will not regret your decision to take part in tonight's... activity. Now before I commence, there are just a few preliminaries. During the meeting we must hold hands across the table. I am the channel, you see, through which your friend can reach you. Once I have moved into my trance in order to get in touch with the Other Side, you must not at any time let go of my hand. Not only will it break the contact, but it could be very dangerous for us both.'

'Dangerous?'

'By breaking contact suddenly, the spirit might be left in limbo and therefore it would have to seek refuge, a host, which would be either myself the transmitter as it were, or yourself, the receiver.' He smiled his oily smile again. 'Such a shock could kill.'

Kate flinched at the word. 'I had no idea this would be so dangerous.'

'Fear not, Mrs Barlow. As long as we keep contact, there is no risk whatsoever. I have been doing this for many years and I'm still here. Now then are we ready?'

Reluctantly, Kate gave a stiff little nod.

'Very good, my dear. Now I must ask you to make your mind a complete blank. Wipe from it all other thoughts and images. Think of it as a sheet of pure white paper. When you have done that, I want you to gradually build up a picture in your mind of the person you wish to contact... and hold it there. Is that clear?'

'Yes.'

Crabtree sat opposite Kate across the table and held his hands out for hers. Trying not to show her revulsion, she placed her hands in his sweaty palms. He clasped them in a firm grip.

'Right, Jean, I think we may begin," Crabtree said softly.

Jean went across to the small upright piano in the corner of the room and began playing quietly. It was a strange discordant piece with no discernible melody. To Kate it seemed as though the music filled the room, the notes resounding in her own head like tidal spray.

Crabtree closed his eyes, muttered a few unintelligible words to himself and then began breathing heavily, his plump shoulders rising and falling in a vigorous rhythm.

The music flooded Kates's senses, the odd chords and harsh melodies creating an image of a sharply defined landscape of black and white hills in her mind. Try as she might she was unable to wipe this vision away to create the pure-white blankness she needed to build up a picture of Michael. Ragged angular rocks imposed themselves against a searing white sky. The rocks glistened with wetness, thrusting hard against the black horizon. Gradually the music seemed to change, growing sweeter, more melodic. The pattern of the rocks changed too: they became smoother, rounder. And then in odd crevices grass and strange plants began to flourish.

The music began to raise her spirits. She felt happy. Joyful. Warm pleasure flooded her body. The music swelled in glorious rhapsody, sweeping her with delight. There were green sprouts everywhere. Lush verdant pastures replaced the rocks which flourished under skies of vibrant blue.

As the music softened, she became conscious of Crabtree's harsh breathing. It grew louder and more regular.

And then suddenly it stopped. A brief aching silence was followed by gagging sounds and fierce cries and then a series of violent exclamations in voices and sometimes languages not his own. These reached a climax in a high unintelligible shout as his body twisted in pain before falling backwards in his chair, jerking Kate forward across the table as he did so.

Beyond the rim of the light, his face appeared featureless like a mannequin in a shop window. Crabtree's voice came to her, harsh and guttural, but his lips did not move.

'Call him. Call him,' it said.

She opened her mouth but no sound came forth. Her throat was dry and cracked. She hadn't spoken for a thousand years.

'Call him!' The plea was urgent.

'Michael,' she croaked. And then more loudly: 'Michael.'

There was silence. A sharp fierce silence like sudden deafness. Although she couldn't see her, Kate was aware that the woman was still playing the piano—but no sound of it could be heard.

The silence pressed against her ears until it hurt.

She called his name again; and heard her own voice echo faintly in the hush. And then...

'Kate'

Ice filled her veins.

'Kate.' It came again. His voice. There could be no mistake. It was no trick, no impersonation; it was Michael.

'My darling Kate.'

She was alone in a dark void. Crabtree had gone, the weird woman playing the piano had gone, the parlour had gone. As she glared into the blackness, she became aware of a pinpoint of light in the far distance. It was moving towards her, growing in size and intensity, burning up the dark. As it grew larger, it began to take shape, a recognisable shape, a man shape.

Michael.

The shape held out its arms to her, the hands squirming, reaching to touch but Kate instinctively held back. She knew it would be wrong to respond to it physically. Words reverberated in her head, her own unspoken thoughts asking forgiveness—a plea to be left in peace.

Michael's voice crowded in on her words, filling her mind, crushing all her thoughts and ideas. 'I want you Kate', the voice boomed. 'I want you.'

'Michael, no, it's too late. It's impossible. If you love me, let me go. Leave me in peace.'

'No. It is not impossible. I can come back. I'm nearly there.'

'NO!' This time she screamed the words out loud.

The features darkened and the eyes blazed. It was not just the expression which soured, but the shape of the face altered as well. Slowly it seemed to buckle with age, the flesh crinkled and fell from the face in long moist slivers until all that was left was the grinning skull, glistening with slime.

'You have no choice in this, Kate,' the skull said, moving towards her.

She gave a sharp cry of terror and closed her eyes, but even then she had a vivid image of the skull. It grew and the darkness of the socket-less eyes engulfed her. She felt heavy with fear; her veins and arteries seemed to be clogging up as though rigor mortis were setting in. With great effort she prised her eyes open. She was back in Crabtree's parlour once more.

The medium was slumped, still in a trance, in the shadows beyond the circle of light. The piano was still being played by his 'helper'. All seemed the same as it had been; and yet it wasn't.

Kate felt uneasy. There was something different—something wrong.

Then she saw it.

***

Timothy couldn't sleep. His head was full to bursting with thoughts of his father. He lay on his back listening to the snores and whispers of the other boys in the dormitory and watching the shadows cast by the trees outside as they shifted in the night breeze. They made interesting shapes on the wall.

***

Michael, or rather his rotting corpse was sitting at the table to Kate's right. He smiled. The grey putrid skin wrinkled around his mouth revealing a black aperture where his teeth had been. Maggots writhed on the top of his skull, their foul bodies slithering down the forehead and landing on the table.

'Ask him what he wants.' The words came from Crabtree, but his mouth did not move. 'Go on, ask him!'

Kate formed the words slowly, forcing them from her dry throat. 'Michael... what is it that you want?'

The eye in the corpse's head glowed with animal fire. The foul mouth opened to speak, expelling the noxious stench of the grave.

'Life, that's what I want. LIFE!'

His spider-like hand reached across the table towards her and Crabtree's leaving a fine trail of slime in its wake. Kate tensed, her heart almost ceasing to beat as the corpse's hand clamped itself over hers. She felt the cold moist texture press against her skin producing an obscene sucking noise. She fought back the overpowering feeling of nausea and wrenched her hand a way from Crabtree's grasp in revulsion.

Time stood still for a moment as she sat transfixed in horror at what she had done.

Too late. The corpse gurgled with delight.

Crabtree gave an agonised gasp, his own hands flying to his throat as though he were being strangled by an unseen force. His corpulent body writhed and twisted wildly like some crazy marionette. As if by some invisible power, he was then lifted out of his chair and propelled with great speed to the corner of the room where he crashed against the wall. Still clutching his throat, he dragged himself to his feet, while his whole body rippled and contorted. He stumbled forward to the table, his eyes bulging from a purple face. With a final flagging scream, he fell forward on to the table vomiting forth a stream of thick green bile.

Kate sat petrified in her chair, transfixed by this hideous pantomime. She saw now that Crabtree's features had changed virtually beyond recognition and his eyes... his eyes contained no pupils.

Kate bit her fist in terror. God, let this nightmare end. It was a nightmare: it could not be real. This could not be happening.

Then, suddenly, Crabtree slid backwards onto the floor and strangely an air of serenity filled the room.

Quietly, Crabtree laughed.

It was a small gentle laugh.

It was Michael's laugh.

And then the medium stopped breathing.

**

As the headlights of Rob Moore' car illuminated briefly the front of his house, drunk as he was, he could see the place was in darkness. He glanced at the clock on the dashboard and as he did so, he dragged the wheel to his left causing the car to scrape against the garden wall.

'Shit!' he cried and stamped on the brake. Stumbling from the car he examined the damage.

'Shit!' he said again as he saw the multiple lines of scratched paint. He kicked the front tyre in anger and then suddenly smiled. So he was still in this world. Little concerns still bothered him. Well, that was something.

'You can stay here until morning,' he growled at the car and staggered towards the house. What had the clock said? Eleven o'clock. Fiona must be out; it was too early for her to be in bed. But as he tried the door, found to his surprise that it was unlocked.

'Curiouser and fucking curiouser,' he mumbled as he tottered over the threshold.

'Fiona,' he cried. 'Fiona, darling, your husband is home—pissed as usual. Aren't you coming to say hello to him?'

He waited for some moments in the dark hall until his words died away.

'Ah well, sod you, I'll have another drinkie.'

He clicked on the lights in the sitting room and what he saw there sobered him up immediately. He staggered backwards, wetting himself as he gazed in horror. Lying on the rug by the fire, circled by a neat pool of dark red blood, was the severed head of his wife.

SEVEN

David clicked off the television and stared at the blank screen. He might as well do that, it was just as interesting as the programme he'd just been watching—but then he hadn't been concentrating. His thoughts had been in a state of turmoil since his interview with Nelson Parker that afternoon.

'We're going to have to ditch your resurrection idea, I'm afraid,' the big man had said across the wide executive desk, a symbol of his importance which he used as a barrier to keep minions at bay.

'Oh, why is that?'

'Ross McGary, the actor who played Margo's husband is dead.'

'Dead. Are you sure?'

'Well, I've spoken to his agent and he should know.'

David frowned. 'That is a turn up for the book. How did it happen?'

'Suicide. Apparently after leaving the show, the poor sod couldn't get any work apart from a few walk ons and some walk overs.'

'I see.'

'It seems the family were able to keep his death from the press or we would have seen it served up as a nice juicy titbit in the tabloids: 'Sacked Soap Star's Sad Suicide'.

'Yes,' said David suddenly feeling very tired.

'One minute you're in a thriving family business two nights a week in all regions and next—you're dead meat.' Parker paused to light a cigarette. 'So I'm afraid that kills your idea of resurrecting John Doyle stone dead.'

David nodded.

'I mean we don't want to extend the viewers' credibility any further; say that he's had plastic surgery to alter his appearance and bring in another actor. Even the cretins who watch the show won't wear that.'

'You don't seem too upset about it.'

'I'm not. In fact, I'm rather pleased because—just between you and me—really don't want Vernon and Sons to survive.'

'Oh.'

Nelson Parker leaned back and gave David one of his knowing glances.

'Come on, David. You are a shrewd cookie. You know as well as I do that V and S is tripe—but what is worse is that it's old-fashioned tripe. It ran out of steam years ago. It's now fading completely from the ratings and has no street cred whatsoever.'

'So all that talk this morning...'

'I was obeying orders and going through the motions. Believe me, Vernon and Sons will be dead and buried by spring.'

'I see.'

Parker shook his head. 'No, no that's where you are wrong. You do not see. Look, when V and S sinks from view there will be a gap in the schedules—a key spot waiting for some up to the minute hard-biting replacement.'

'And you have got such a replacement?'

Parker beamed and wriggled in his chair in smug pleasure.

'Bright boy. I will have it and I want you in on the ground floor.'

'Really.'

'Is that all you can say?'

'I can't say more until I know more.'

'That's fair enough.' Parker chuckled and then stubbing out his cigarette cast a keen glance at David. 'Right: provisional title is 'Cop Shop'. A police station in one of our inner cities—maybe Birmingham. It will follow the lives of the police officers on and off duty. There will be plenty of scope to include all the topical issues, current concerns etc. Half the cast will be permanent and the other half will be transient, giving us opportunities for guest appearances and big name cameos. I'd like you to mould the format into shape and head the writing team. Are you interested?'

Of course he was interested. This was what he had longed for: to be in at the creation of a high-profile programme. He'd realised long before that shoring up the failing fortunes of Vernon and Sons would bring no kudos; although, ironically, it must have been his work on this that had led to Parker's offer.

Since the interview, David's mind had been swimming with ideas and he longed to tell Kate the good news. It was possible that she could be written into the show and this mutual interest would help to secure their new and brighter future. Cue the strings and bring on the sunset. He grinned. But dammit it was true. Working together would help to forge a firmer partnership and eradicate the bad memories, memories of Michael from their lives.

David suddenly realised that he didn't want to lose Kate. It was a revelation. It finally came home to him that he not only wanted her but needed her. My God, he thought, is this it then? Is this love with a capital L? He had always known there was something special about Kate, but now it seemed he was being forced into the responsibility of loving her. No, that wasn't quite true. His feelings had not suddenly changed; it was only that he had found a name for them. What was really new was that the thought of it no longer frightened him; in fact, he felt good.

He glanced at his watch. Nearly eleven. Where was she? Then he grinned. He knew that having dinner with a director was often more ordeal than pleasure and often ran into extra time. If it was doing Kate and her career some good, he could wait, impatient as he was.

He stretched himself luxuriously and drank in the quiet of the cottage. All was still and peaceful. He grinned again. At last things seemed to be going right.

***

For some moments Rob stood transfixed, his mind failing to come to terms with what he saw. This must be some kind of monstrous practical joke: a latex head, tomato sauce...

The dead glazed eyes of Fiona Moore stared unseeing at him, the mouth slightly open as in surprise. Her blond hair trailed in the dark pool of congealed blood which circled the head.

With a few faltering steps, Rob moved to the head and leaning forward allowed his fingers to touch the skin. It was cold and hard, but it was real.

Dead meat. Rob retched and, turning quickly away, he was violently sick.

Moments later, wiping the tears away, he gazed at his wife's decapitated head. He knew now that the nightmare had finally taken over. He was no longer in touch with reality. The madness had claimed him. He cried uncontrollably, his body racked with sobs. After a time, a stoical quietness finally overcame him, and the deadness of spirit settled down within him. It was then, as a chilling numbness overtook the pain, that the thought struck him: where the hell was the body—where was the rest of his wife? Slowly he scanned the room; but it wasn't there. As in a trance he began to search the downstairs rooms as in some ghoulish game of hunt the body. He moved slowly and methodically through the stillness of the house without the full emotional comprehension of his task.

Finally, he peered up into the darkness at the top of the stairs and with an instinctive realisation, he knew Fiona was in their bedroom. She would be lying there, waiting to be discovered. As he mounted the stairs towards the encroaching darkness, he began to feel a dull ache in his heart.

Not daring to turn the light on, he felt his way along the landing and into the bedroom. There sprawling diagonally across the bed was the headless corpse of his wife. Splatters of blood were everywhere. Rob was now drained of all emotion and reaction. He just gazed dully at the bed, the pain in his heart growing stronger, like cramped fingers squeezing each ventricle. Creamy moonlight spilling into the room dusted the body with pale frosting, giving it the appearance of some large theatrical doll.

And then from the shadows he heard a low mirthless laugh. It cut through the silence like a sword. It came again louder and harsher. It was a laugh he knew. It was a laugh he expected. It was a laugh from his nightmares, only this time there was no waking up.

Once more the laugh spewed into the darkness, the darkness that still shrouded its owner. He was the master of Rob's nightmares and he had come to claim him.

***

'He's dead. He's dead.' Jean Wilson knelt by the body of Arthur Crabtree and moaned. 'Arthur, it's Jean.' She leaned close to the still white face. 'Speak to me Arthur.'

Kate looked on as though she were watching a play. The scene she had witnessed had no connection with her. It was being acted out by strangers wanting to achieve some gruesome dramatic effect. In this it had been successful: it had terrified and nauseated her but thankfully it wasn't real. How could it be? It had been fantastic. However, now she'd had enough of this entertainment and it was time for her to go. To get the hell out of there. With stiff and unsteady legs, she stood to leave—as she did so, Jean Wilson, disturbed by her movements, turned her moist eyes to Kate. They narrowed to a vicious slit.

'Yes.' The word was almost a grunt. She moved towards Kate, her dull tear-blotched face twisted with hate. 'You are to blame for this,' she growled pointing an accusing finger. 'If it wasn't for you, Arthur would be alive. You've killed him!'' She lunged at Kate, pushing her back against the table with a crash.

'Please, no,' gasped Kate, winded by the attack. The woman now seemed to have lost control and had turned into a manic harpy. She grappled ferociously with Kate, the coarse hands reaching for her throat. It was the blindness of the attack that allowed Kate, who was the stronger of the two, to thrust her away.

'Stop it' she cried. 'Pull yourself together.' Kate realised that now she was playing a part in this weird drama, dragged as it were over the footlights. The words were not her own, just her lines: the remembered clichés. 'No one is to blame. He knew the risks. I didn't ask for this.' She slotted these fragments of dialogue into a coherent statement. 'I didn't ask for this,' she repeated, making a wide gesture as she did so, to indicate the set. Her hand knocked against the lightshade sending fierce shadows swinging across the room.

The woman playing Jean Wilson had fallen back and was once more crouching over the body of Arthur Crabtree, her fit of fury over.

'It must have been his heart; some kind of heart attack.' Kate continued, 'You'll need to contact a doctor to confirm that. And now I must be going.'

With the cool confidence that the part demanded, she straightened her coat and walked slowly from the room. The Wilson creature looked after her for a few moments as though mesmerised by Kate's performance, then turning back to the inert form of Arthur Crabtree, she fell upon his body with a moan of despair.

Calmly Kate left the house, buttoning up her coat against the sharp night air as she did so. It was all very ordinary. She slipped casually into the driving seat and showed no surprise when the car started without any difficulty. She gave no final glance back at the peeling green door or a thought to what she had just experienced on the other side of it. She just revved the engine and drove off.

After driving for some five minutes, it began to happen. At first, she started to shiver. Her armour of pretence started to buckle under mental pressure and the reality of the séance pierced her consciousness. She was ice-cold and shivering so much that she could hardly keep her hands on the wheel. The oncoming headlights began to blur into one amorphous brightness. Kate heard noises too, loud fierce wailing noises. Car horns. Blaring. Searing. The light seemed to be coming towards her—to engulf her. Momentarily her brain cleared and with chilling realisation, she saw she was in the wrong lane. The bright lights burning down on her were the headlights of an oncoming vehicle. A large oncoming vehicle.

Desperately she swung the steering wheel over and with squealing tyres, the car rocked violently and slewed across to the other side of the road, out of her control. A large hedge sprang up into the full glare of her headlights. Skeletally spiky, it advanced towards the car at great speed. Kate was too slow to react. Her mind was confused and dull as though the cogs of thought had jammed. She just felt so cold.

The car tore through the hedge and seemed to Kate to shoot up into the dark void of space. There was a sensation of flying. And blackness was all around. Indeed, blackness was spilling into the car: she welcomed it. She was glad to feel its inky warmth as it enveloped her, caressing her, just before she felt the pain.

***

'Hello Rob. Did you like my little surprise?'

The voice was thick and guttural but still recognisable as that belonging to Michael Barlow. It came from the grey shadows of the bedroom.

The taunting smug tone created an edgy tension inside Rob and snapped any self-reserve he had, 'Let's see you, you bastard,' he barked. 'Let me see you, you murdering bastard!'

'With pleasure,' came the rasping reply.

A table lamp snapped on, bathing the room in pale light—it was a light that dispelled shadows and softened contours.

'Satisfied?' said the voice, the owner of which could now be seen clearly.

Rob did not know exactly what he had expected. Michael was dead, for God's sake and although he had seen his face, his dead face, leer close to him in his dreams, nothing in his imagination had come close to the horror that faced him now.

Standing in the corner of the bedroom, smiling, was the rotting corpse of Michael Barlow, the tatters of a suit hung from the decaying body; the face was virtually fleshless, but small patches of putrescence which had once been skin clung to the slimy skull. Both eye sockets were now dark voids. The thing however was breathing: the shallow rib cage rose and fell emitting a thick gurgling sound and, as it opened its mouth, the foul stench of rot was expelled.

'Not a pretty sight, eh?' said the thing, shambling a little closer to Rob.

'What are you?' Rob asked as he felt his brain shutting down. The corpse held out an arm to touch him. He flinched and pulled back.

'That's no way to treat an old friend; and let's face it, Robby, you and I are old friends. We share many memories together. Do you remember?'

Rob closed his eyed and groaned. One tattered vestige of his mind clung on to the wild hope that this indeed was another of his crazy nightmares.

'I'd better warn you,' the thing continued as though interpreting this thought, 'I am not a figment of your imagination. This is real. I'm here. I've got through at last.'

Rob now felt totally adrift from his reason. He shook his head as if to shake his addled senses back to sanity. 'You're dead. Why come back? What are you after?'

'To settle a few old scores, shall we say. And for Kate.'

'Is this what you mean by settling old scores?' Rob turned, his fear converting to anger as he pointed to Fiona's dismembered corpse on the bed.

'Yes, Rob. I thought you'd like my handiwork. Oh, the number of times you told me you how trapped you felt with Fiona. How she disappointed you as a wife. How you longed to be free of her.' The creature laughed, its obscene chest rippling with the effort and the dark mucus dripping from the corners of the mouth.

'Well, I've done the job for you. Now you're free of her. You're on your own at last. No more nagging Fiona.'

The truth of this statement overwhelmed Rob and he felt a dry gagging sensation in his throat. Fiery tears pricked his eyes as he sank wearily on to the corner of the bed.

'Yes, Rob, old boy.' Michael's voice was soft and smug. 'I suspect that now you realise that, in fact, Fiona was your support. Your crutch. The truth was that it was you who held her back. You were the one who needed her like a blind man needs a white stick. That is the truth. I knew it a long time ago. A pity you didn't. But you know now don't you, Rob, old boy? Don't you?'

Rob Moore's supply of words had dried up. He had no coherent response. It was all true what this thing had said. Oh, he had known before but had kept it locked in a corner of his mind and only occasionally had he unlocked it to examine, usually when he was depressed or drunk—or both.

On later reflection he would always deny what he knew was the truth. And the truth was that he had been the one who had destroyed the marriage. Fiona had not only supported him in the early days but made sacrifices in her own career so that he could climb up the greasy pole in Television Land. And in the end, he had been the one to shut her out, to cast her aside for a series of trite and tasteless affairs with empty-headed secretaries and bimbo starlets. He had been the real bastard. Poor Fiona had been the victim. No wonder she turned away from him and became… what did he call her? The ice maiden. And yet in her own way, she still stood by him. What a prize arsehole he was. And it was this decaying corpse creature standing before him now that had caused him to really face the truth at last.

My God, what was happening to his world? Everything was disintegrating. Logic had been blown away. Here was dead Michael Barlow standing before him in the flesh—the rotting flesh. 'The time has been that, when the brains were out, the man would die and there an end.' What did it all mean? Why had he been dragged out of the real world into this hellish parody of life where the dead walked—and killed.

One question did spring into his ravaged mind to ask the fiend that now confronted him.

'What do you want of me?'

'Ah, I'm glad you asked me that. It saves me having to raise the rather delicate subject myself.'

The mock politeness and reasonableness by which this creature talked increased Rob's sense of insanity, creating further erosion of his crumbling mental structures.

'I feel rather like Cinderella.' Michael continued, his breath still thick and heavy as though every word had to fight its way out of the dead mouth. 'You see, like old Cinders, I want to go to the ball, but as you can observe, I have nothing to wear.

However, you, Rob, my old friend, shall be my fairy godmother and provide the necessities.'

Rob frowned and the corpse shook once more with merriment. The dark eyeless sockets bored into him.

'In simple terms, I want your body. I can hardly move around like this. It's hardly decent. So you see in your dying minutes you will be playing a most significant role in my resurrection.'

***

He was on a cross, arms outstretched in the classic pose. Nails were being hammered into the palms of his hands. They sank into the soft white flesh but there was no pain; only the sound of the hammering bothered him.

Bang. Bang. Bang.

The noise ricocheted around his brain.

Bang. Bang. Bang.

He screwed up his eyes, eclipsing the view of the violence being done to his hands, but in the darkness the hammer blows sounded louder.

Bang. Bang. Bang.

He woke.

The hammer blows continued.

Bang. Bang. Bang.

Full consciousness flooded over him. Someone at the door. David struggled up from his sprawled position and staggered towards the knocking. He caught a glance at the clock. Nearly one. It must be Kate. Can't find her key again. God, she's late.

Bang. Bang Bang.

'Coming my lovely,' he called in a silly voice, warming with anticipation of seeing her again. He slipped the catch and pulled back the door allowing the dim amber light of the hall to spill out on to the porch, where a dark shape was waiting for him. It wasn't Kate.

'Good evening, sir.' said the figure in blue. 'May I come in?'

***

Timothy Barlow was fighting it: the strange feeling that was invading his body. He wanted to scream out with uncertainty and fear. But he didn't want to be removed from his dormitory again; he didn't want to gain a reputation for being odd. They could be very cruel to you at St. Austell's if you were odd.

His body was chilling up as though he had been injected with ice crystals. And there were cramps in his legs. He bit his lip as he squirmed in distress trying to control the spasms of pain. Whatever happened he must not disturb the other boys who were now filling the air with the heavy breathing of sleep. In time the discomfort would go away and then in the morning everything would be normal again.

At the far end of the dormitory a door opened and a sharp rectangle of yellow light slid into the room.

Silhouetted there was a tall slim figure. A torch beam flashed.

Tim forced himself to lie still.

The prefect crossed the threshold, his shoes producing an eerie clipping sound on the parquet floor like some phantom horse. The torch beam swept crazily across the room, falling briefly on Tim's bed.

He held his breath, his body coiled in anticipation. The rough blanket felt like the rasp of sandpaper on his sensitive skin, but he did not move.

The torch beam moved on; and then like a film playing in reverse, the figure, after a moment's pause, retreated backwards, snapping off the torch before closing the door.

Hot tears sprang to Timothy's eyes as he flung himself on his back and dug his nails into the palms of his hands. Outside a cruel moon shone down uncaringly as the scent of evil floated abroad.

**

'How did it happen?'

'Difficult to say, sir. An eye-witness said that she just seemed to lose control of the vehicle. It veered right across the road, mounted the pavement, smashed through a hedge and down a thirty feet drop. The car was a write-off. It's a miracle she wasn't killed on impact.'

'My God.' David put his head in his hands. He felt weak with shock. Tiredness began to weigh down on him. He just wanted to go back to sleep, to hide in the warm security of unconsciousness. And then a painful thought flashed into his mind. 'She's not dead is she? You're not trying to break this to me gently are you?'

The eyes in the expressionless face of the policeman flickered for a moment; he spoke in low matter-of-fact tones. 'No, sir, but she is in a bad way. As I said before, she's in Intensive Care.'

'I must see her.'

The policeman nodded. 'We can run you to the hospital now.'

'No, no, I'll go myself.'

'Are you sure you're in a fit state?' the policeman said looking pointedly at the half-empty bottle of scotch on the coffee table.

A touch of irritation reared in the numbness of David's senses. 'Of course I'm capable. I've only had one drink. Do you want to breathalyse me?' He found his voice rising in anger.

'I was just thinking about the emotional upset, sir. You've had quite a shock to your system.'

David ran his fingers through his hair. 'Yes, I'm sorry... I'm just not thinking straight.'

'I understand, sir. Now are you sure that we can't run you down to the hospital. It'd be no trouble.' The policeman rose, his raincoat rustling unnaturally in the quiet.

'No. Thank you all the same. I'd prefer to go on my own.' David forced a smile. 'Don't worry, I'll be all right.'

'Very well, sir. We'll be in touch with you presently regarding the accident, but I'll leave you now so you can get off to the hospital.' He retreated to the door and then turned back briefly. 'I hope everything works out OK,'

David nodded dumbly. He didn't trust himself to speak. A well of sadness and despair was rising up inside him. He somehow knew this was the end of it all. Kate would never regain consciousness. She would die leaving him feeling guilty and alone. And only a few hours earlier he had been predicting the golden dawn of their new life. And now...

He stood for a moment unable to move locked in his own thoughts and then the sound of the police car starting up and driving off broke his reverie. He must get to Kate. Quickly.

Whatever was going to happen, he must be with her.

***

Rob knew he was dying. He could feel it and strangely enough it didn't frighten him. Had he been able to consider fully the implications of what was happening to him, he probably would have felt the same. Life held nothing for him now. He had glimpsed hell and its horrors, and he welcomed the embrace of the great oblivion—the blessed peace.

The remnant of Michael Barlow came closer to him, breathing the foul stink of death—the smell of sulphur, rot and decay. The dark eye sockets held him in thrall, transfixed to the bed while life was slowly being sucked out of him.

Rob felt the power of movement fading as though controls were being switched off in various parts of his body. Already his lower half was paralysed: no feeling, no function, nothing. He had lost the use of his fingers also. They were just sticks of lifeless bone and tissue.

Then the arms.

A chilling cold gripped his body where sensation was left and then, incredibly, he could feel his heartbeat slowing down. It was then that a kind of panic gripped him. He must speak before his mouth and vocal chords were struck by the creeping malaise of death.

'Why are you doing this? What do you want?' His mouth moved in slow motion, the words emerging in a slurred fashion as though he was very drunk.

'I can hardly start my new life as I am,' came the reply. 'What would people say?'

The thing that had been Michael Barlow gurgled with delight. 'As I said, I need new clothes for my body, or to be more precise, I need a new body.'

Rob opened his mouth to say more, but it remained open, slack and useless. The tongue was now lifeless. For a moment his eyes flashed wildly, the brain carrying the full burden of panic for the now dormant body; and then came the final inexorable blackness.

Like a marionette with severed strings, the body of Rob Moore slumped back on to the bed, his arms spilling loosely across the cover close to the corpse of his wife.

For a moment there was stillness. The scene was held, like a madman's painting.

And then the body began to move once more. The flesh started to ripple and undulate like the throbbing of some life-sized maggot. Hands twitched and the head seemed to expand, balloon-like forcing the eyelids open and exposing the bulbous whites of the eyes.

A gargling and gurgling sound issued from the throat while green bile escaped in a fine trickle from the corners of the mouth. The noise rose in intensity gradually transforming into a loud human cry, which wracked the whole body causing it to thrash about the bed as though caught in the throes of some violent fit.

Then, once again, there was stillness.

In that bedroom, with the creamy moonlight still falling through the window on to the inert forms of Rob Moore and his wife, there was quiet. The grotesque replica of Michael Barlow was gone. The only evidence of his having been there was a putrid mess by the side of the bed and several ragged shreds of clothing scattered by it.

After some moments in that silence, that awful silence, the inert figure stirred. The chest rose and fell in quick succession. Rob Moore was breathing again.

Slowly but with ease the body sat up. The eyes flickered open; the pupils gradually settled into a wide fixed stare. They were those familiar sardonic eyes but somehow different.

The face grinned and laughed. It was an unfamiliar laugh. The shell of Rob Moore had accepted its new tenant.

**

Far away across the darkness of England, in the darkness before the streaks of dawn lighten the sky, Timothy Barlow screamed.

EIGHT

David loathed hospitals. He had never been a patient in one himself, but he hated them instinctively. To him, they made one confront the reality of death. Here was the incontrovertible evidence of the mortality of man. Here amid these white sheets and hushed corridors were rooms crammed with the ill and dying. They were the domain of twisted, damaged bodies, haggard faces and bedridden creatures with were being destroyed from within. There was something wrong with your world if you were in hospital, even as a visitor, as he was now, for you were helpless. All one could do is to watch the healing or the decay on the sidelines—like some ghoulish spectator sport.

There was about the phrase Intensive Care, he thought as he entered the cocooned world of the hospital, something that made you lower your voice when speaking the words. A ritual utterance that allowed one to be ushered into the sanctum of the terminally ill. A staff nurse led him down the long polished corridors with the squeaky floors and dim lighting, dotted at regular intervals with reminders of illness, diseases and death: people in wheel-chairs, on stretchers, with walking-frames, being helped to totter, in grim dressing gowns, from one place to another. As a patient in such places, you had to leave dignity at the door.

They reached the private side ward where Kate was. The nurse asked him to wait outside a moment while she went in and checked how things were. Moments dragged by. Hushed hospital moments that almost anaesthetized the senses. The pervasive antiseptic smell assailed his nostrils causing his head to throb with the power of it. His mouth grew dry and his stomach queasy as though all parts of him were being invaded by the antiseptic stench of attempted healing.

At length a ward sister in dark blue appeared with a starched rustle and tight regulation smile. 'Mr. Cole? Hello,' she purred softly. 'Are you the husband?'

No, I'm the lover.

'No, her husband is dead. I'm a close friend.'

The sharp eyes of the sister prompted him for further information. He didn't give it. With a dead husband already established, he wasn't about to identify himself as 'her partner'. It would do little for Kate's standing as a patient.

'May I see her?'

A hesitation and then: 'Very well. But only for a moment. She is unconscious, of course. She's in a state of shock. There is some internal bleeding and at present we do not know the extent of her injuries. We will have to wait until her condition stabilises before we can carry out further examinations.'

The words just flowed over David's head. He just wanted to see her. He said so again.

When he did see her, he cried. Spontaneously and unselfconsciously, he cried. It was an awful sight: Kate lay in a high-sided cot like a giant baby. Her face was deathly white, her dark hair scraped back showing the purple and amber bruises and blood spots near the hairline. She had tubes coming out of her mouth, nose and arm. Her hands were bandaged and laid down delicately by her side. This wasn't Kate. This wasn't the woman he knew. This was some kind of Frankenstein's monster.

He wiped away the tears with his sleeve and leaned over the bars of the cot, 'Kate', he said softly.

The body lay still, the face frozen as in death.

David had striven all his life to be in command of his own situation - to control and arrange things as he wanted them. That was one reason why he'd never married. That kind of commitment spelt doom to his kind of independence. What he was only just coming to realise was that it wasn't the legal commitment that stifled the spirit of self-sufficiency but the emotional one—and unknowingly he had made one to Kate. So now he was helpless. He knew that he could not say or do anything which could change, influence or ease the situation. This is what happens when you care for someone. This sensation of helplessness was almost as painful as seeing Kate as she was now.

'Mr Cole.'

It was the voice of the ward sister.

'I think you'd better leave now. If you'd like to call in the morning, say around ten, when Mr Morrison will be on duty.'

'Will she die?' He cut through the practical protocol with his words, although he asked the question in a matter of fact manner.

The sister's tired face showed no change of expression. It was a question she had been asked many times of many patients. Experience and her familiarity with death had made her immune to emotional involvement. Inevitably, she had to remain professional.

'She is in a critical condition, Mr Cole, but we are doing all we possibly can to save her. It's early days yet, but there is all to hope for.'

David nodded. The words didn't really mean anything, but they did have some kind of comforting effect. He turned to leave—as he did so the sister gave him a warm smile and touched his arm.

'She's in good hands,' she said simply. David's throat dried and he could hardly force out a reply, he made his way slowly towards the door.

***

Dawn was just stealing into the sky as the door of the Rob Moore's house opened and Rob stepped out. He breathed deeply, taking in the cool, sharp morning air. He stretched and grinned.

It was good to be alive. Again.

***

'Honestly, Matron, I'm OK. It was just a nightmare.'

Matron looked down at the pale features of the youngster in her charge. There was something wrong with this Barlow boy, something which was beyond her experience and something which unnerved her.

She'd had to deal with hundreds of boys who for one reason or another suffered from bad dreams; it was a common enough complaint in a boarding school where children were isolated from love, real caring and the family home—but Timothy Barlow was an exception somehow. She could not forget his odd behaviour of a few days ago and the way he had kissed her. Even the recollection of it made her shudder. That was no little boy's kiss, no matter how precocious he may be. There was something evil about it.

'What was your nightmare about?' she asked, mixing him a mild sedative.

'Nothing, really.'

She gave him a hard look. 'Nonsense. No one screams the place down as you did over nothing. I want to know what your dream was about,' she said tartly, and added as an afterthought: 'Then I can help you.'

Timothy examined his feet.

'Come on, Timothy, you can tell me.' The voice had softened considerably and now resonated with theatrical sweetness. He looked at her almost in disbelief at the changing tactics, the move from threats to coaxing. He knew, however, he would never escape her, never get back to his own dormitory until he supplied her with some story that would satisfy her. He certainly couldn't tell her the truth. He didn't want to share those awful images that invaded his dreams with anyone. To say them out loud might make them come true.

'I was being chased,' he said. 'I was chased by a hairy monster.' He paused a moment and then warming to his task, he added, 'It had one eye in the middle of his head, and it trapped me in a dark cave and I couldn't get out.'

By Matron's expression, he could see that she didn't believe him. She knew he was lying—but how could she prove it? He added a few more gory details to the story before she stopped his flow by putting the drink in his hand.

'Drink this and then go back to your dormitory. It's nearly time to get up by now anyway.' She said briskly, all the softness having evaporated her voice. The boy was a nuisance and a liar. Why it bothered her so, she could not tell. She just felt disturbed by him.

'If you have any more nightmares about big hairy monsters, we shall have to contact your parents.'

'Parent,' Tim corrected. 'My father is dead.'

***

It was almost dawn when David arrived back at the cottage. He made no attempt to go to bed. There was no point: it was too late now, and he certainly wouldn't sleep. He made himself a cup of black coffee and sat in the kitchen watching the fingers of the morning draw pink-red scratches across the sky. The scalding coffee burnt his throat and warmed him but he didn't feel anything. He was just numbed by the recent events.

All was still and quiet apart from the far-off sound of the sea and the clicking and knocking of the central heating radiators as they warmed up.

David glanced at his watch: it was already after eight. He ought to shower and change. By then it would be nearly time for him to return to the hospital and see the doctor. He wandered up towards the bathroom trying not to think of Kate, but the image, that awful image of her strapped in that monstrous crib, came floating insistently into his mind. He stood for a moment on the landing, screwing up his eyes in some attempt to shake away this vision from his mind. As he did so, a sharp sound caught his attention. His eyes flew open and he held himself tensely as he listened. The noise came again. It was the door of Michael's studio which was flapping open as though caught in some errant draught—except there was no draught.

He was drawn to that damned room once again and without thinking, he entered. It was still a chilling place but he felt no threat here now. The oppression he had experienced before had somehow evaporated. In daylight there seemed no sense of danger anymore. He felt the air leaving his lungs, suddenly realising how tense he had been.

Quietly relaxed now, he began to survey the room with its damaged paintings and then he began to grow angry. Hatred swelled up inside him; a boiling hatred of Michael Barlow, for the misery he had caused Kate and for the happiness he had denied her. And anger, too, for whoever controls our lives; God—or whatever you wanted to call the celestial puppet master. They had been played with, Kate and he, as in some great sneering supernatural game of torture. Build 'em up so's you can knock 'em down. Just as Kate was starting to leave behind the pain caused by that blasted husband of hers, this had to happen.

He clenched his fists. He did not want to give vent to violence. That was foolish... but, yes, he did want to do some hurt, some damage. It wouldn't solve anything but it would give him dome perverse satisfaction. His pent up emotions demanded some release. The painting—yes—the smug portrait of that bastard, Michael. He would rip that malevolent self-satisfied grin from its face.

Scanning the room, his eyes found the portrait which lay on the floor close to the easel. The surface shimmered and glared with the early morning light which fell on it from the skylight above. As David gazed down at it, detail was hard to see. He kicked it with his foot to alter the position, but it made no difference to the surface sheen which seemed to shield the face from David's scrutiny. Faintly through the brilliance, he could just make out the vague outline of Michael's features; as he did so, his anger seemed to dissipate. There was no point in venting his fury on an inanimate canvas. The power of Michael, sick as it was, worked through the memories and minds of the people who knew him, not through a painting of the man.

He picked it up and examined it closely. The painted face stared blankly back at him. It had lost vibrancy and power to menace. The features were now set in innocent repose. Indeed, as the cumulus clouds hurried by outside, shifting the patterns of light in the studio, the expression worn by the face of Michael Barlow, it seemed to David, was one of contentment.

***

The blue car with the scratched paintwork on the offside wing pulled into the car park of 'The Busy Bee' transport cafe. It looked oddly dwarfed by the side of the juggernauts and container lorries already parked there. It was some moments after the engine was switched off that the driver of the blue car emerged. He was still smiling and still taking in gulps of the fresh morning air. He was hungry. It had been over a year since last he'd eaten. The thought of bacon and eggs swilled down with hot tea thrilled him.

With awkward, jerky movements he made his way in to 'The Busy Bee'. The new body was still strange to him, despite the fact that it was a similar build to his own.

Not to worry, he thought, his grin broadening, this is only a temporary arrangement.

***

As David was buttoning up his clean shirt, he suddenly thought of Tim. What should he do about the boy? If his mother were dying, God forbid, then he ought to be informed. He did not relish the thought of having to do that. But surely these morbid thoughts were premature and certainly it was pointless worrying Tim before there was something definite to tell him. The lad was highly strung as it was - not surprisingly so being the off-spring of such disparate parents. He had his mother's pale delicate features and sensitivity, while inheriting some of his father's moody unpredictability. Certainly since Michael's death this side of the boy's nature had shown itself more.

It was true that in the early days of his relationship with Kate, he had looked on Tim as an encumbrance, a handicap which he had to accept if he were to go on making love to Kate. However, as time passed and he got to know him, he'd grown to like him; although he had never reconciled it in his own mind that this boy was Michael's spawn and there would be forever something alien about him.

What would happen to her son if Kate died, he shuddered to think. But what was worse: what would happen to him if Kate died? That did not bear contemplation.

As he knotted his tie, he looked at himself in the mirror. A pale tired face gazed back at him. A face that was ageing, the charming youthful bloom around the eyes and mouth was fading. Middle-age was marking out a plot development.

He pulled the knot tight and grimaced at himself. Better get back to the hospital. He would decide what to do about Timothy when he'd heard what the doctor had to say and until then he would shut his brain down. No more morbid thoughts. No more thoughts. Normal service will be resumed as soon as possible.

***

Daylight now flooded into the house, exposing each grim horror to clear view. The pool of blood on the living room carpet had crusted over forming a hard crimson base for the severed head which was now a waxy yellow, the skin beginning to pucker. The muscles of the face had slackened letting the jaw drop wide open in a silent scream.

***

Upstairs the torso of Fiona Moore lay on the bed but the remnants of Michael Barlow's corpse had turned into a pile of fine white ash which shifted slightly as the breeze from an open window played with it.

All was silent. Absolute quiet. This was the domain of the dead. The really dead.

***

Jean Wilson pulled Arthur Crabtree upright in the armchair, supporting his body with cushions.

'There now,' she said pleasantly, 'now you're comfortable.'

The white rigid features and dark vacant eyes of the medium looked back at her blankly.

'When I've seen to the fire, I'll make us a nice cup of tea.' She leant forward timidly, her heart fluttering as she placed a gentle kiss on the cold flesh of his forehead.

***

Rob swilled back the last of his tea. He felt good. The meal had warmed him and helped to bring suppleness back to the body. He felt more at home in it now—and more agile.

He glanced at his watch. Time he was going. He felt strangely excited. And why shouldn't he: he was going to see his son again.

***

There was no apparent change in Kate. She lay there in the same position as when he'd first seen her, with the hideous tubes still in place. The skin was alabaster white; the eyes closed; the breathing almost imperceptible. The nurse had tried to reassure David that this was a relatively good sign.

Relatively. Better than no breath at all!

'It shows that her condition is stabilising and she certainly has got no worse since she came in.'

It was a different nurse. She had a pleasant face with a gentle Scottish burr. All very reassuring—but not to him.

He now waited in a cramped little office for the doctor to come and talk to him.

'Ah yes.' He heard the words before he saw the owner: a young man with large sensitive blue eyes and thin sandy hair, his hands dug deeply into the pockets of his dingy white coat.

'Mr...'

'Cole. David Cole.'

'You've come about Mrs Barlow?'

He nodded.

'And you are her...'

'We live together. Her husband is dead.' More honesty this time.

The young doctor nodded. Was there, David thought, a gentle roll of the eye, or did he imagine it? Was he being too sensitive?

'Yes. I see,' the doctor he said, pulling up a chair to sit by David. When he had done so, David could see how young this chap was. Very young. Surely he was not old enough to be capable of treating a serious case like this. It needed someone older, more experienced, less gauche than this youth.

'Well, Mrs Barlow's had a heck of a knock. There is some internal damage, but nothing too serious we think; however the accident has been such a shock to her system that it has sent her into a coma.'

A coma. The words echoed like cannon fire around David's brain.

'Now, don't jump to conclusions, Mr Cole. This is not so bad as it sounds. Her mind has gone into limbo, as it were, in order to protect her body from the pain of the accident. It is not uncommon in such cases and as the body heals and the pain lessens, so the brain realises there is less need to protect itself and then gradually, naturally, the patient comes out of the coma.'

'Will she live?' David wanted simplicity. Basic certainties. He was not interested in processes. He just wanted Kate alive.

The doctor gave a nervous smile. 'I'm afraid I can't deal in guarantees, Mr Cole, but I do believe there is a good chance of her pulling through. The first forty-eight hours are the most crucial.'

The doctor paused for David to make some comment but he remained silent. 'If I were you, I'd go home and try to get some rest. We will contact you if there is any major change in Mrs Barlow's condition.'

David clenched his fist. Why must he keep referring to her as Mrs Barlow. It was Kate he was talking about. Kate. His Kate. Barlow was dead and buried and no longer had any claim on her.

The young doctor stood up. 'If you'll excuse me now, Mr Cole, I am rather busy.'

David nodded, 'Of course. Thank you'. The doctor gave a professional grin of reassurance and left.

So there it was. He must wait. The thing David hated most: waiting. Waiting with all the uncertainty that it brings. That was the shape of his future. And there was nothing he could do to alter the situation.

He must wait.

Lethargically he pulled himself to his feet and left the little office. He spent some moments with Kate, looking down at that immobile pale mask until he could bear it no longer, and began to make his way out of the ward. Before he was able to leave, he was stopped by the pretty Scottish nurse.

'Mr Cole, here are Kate's things, her belongings and such which were pulled out of the car.'

She had used her name, Kate. Bless her for that. He turned and smiled at her, as she held out a large black plastic bag.

'Thank you,' he said taking the bag; and he meant it.

***

Rob Moore pulled his car off the road just before the entrance to the drive. He got out and looked over the hedge at the stark block of buildings half a mile away. St. Austell's School for Boys. He remembered how he and Kate had discussed Tim's education—how they had argued about sending him away. Kate had wanted it very much, he knew, so that Tim would be away from his influence and not able to witness his bouts of irrational, violent behaviour.

St. Austell's School for Boys. Very pukka. Still residing in the 19th century. Masters with gowns, ancient traditions and strict rules. Tom Brown would have felt at home here.

Rob Matthew's face creased into a smile. It had all worked out rather well in the end.

***

Nelson Parker growled in exasperation. What the hell was happening to his workforce?

'Are you sure?' he barked down the telephone.

'I'll try again if you like, but there's no answer.'

Yes. Keep trying.' Both Rob Moore and David Cole had failed to turn up for work that morning and they weren't answering their phones. It was worse than trying to raise the dead.

***

The phone was ringing when David got back to the cottage. As he raced to the receiver, he prayed it was not the hospital with bad news. Sudden turn for the worse. Situation deteriorated. Nothing could be done.

Dead.

It was Nelson Parker's secretary.

'I won't be in today, Gloria?' he said. 'Kate's had an accident. She's in... hospital.'

'Oh, I am sorry,' replied the tinny voice. 'Is it bad?'

David did not know how to answer. He didn't want to confirm his thoughts verbally.

'I'm sorry, I can't talk now. Explain to Nelson for me will you? I'll be in touch soon.'

'Yes, of course.'

He hung up and sank into a chair—drained of energy.

Perhaps he should have gone into the office and tried to work, take his mind off things; but he knew he couldn't have written a bloody word with this sword of Damocles hanging over his head. God, life was cruel. If only Kate had not gone after the part. What had she had to drink at last night? Strange—the police had made no reference to drinking—but what else could it be? She was a good driver, a safe driver. She must have been plied with booze at that dinner last night. What kind of idiot was it that would let someone drive off knowing them to be drunk? What was the name of that sodding director? He'd have something to answer for?

Suddenly, he realised that he didn't know the man. He had no idea who Kate had been with last night... or even where she'd been. The shock of this realisation filled him with a sense of panic. He really knew nothing about what Kate did last night.

His mind raced wildly for some moments before he made an effort to calm himself down. Surely, he told himself, it wouldn't be too difficult to find out where Kate had been. Wait a minute, what was that play called? 'The Spider Trap' wasn't it? Hadn't he seen a copy of the script in the kitchen this morning? Quickly he went through into the kitchen and within moments he had the script in his hand. He flipped through the pages and a piece of notepaper fell out. It had a BBC heading and the name Julian Myles at the top. A scribbled message below read: 'Kate, do give this serious thought. The part of Irene is ideal for you. Ring me. J.'

David did not know Julian Myles, but now was the time to get acquainted. He rang the number and a female voice answered, 'Julian Myles' office, can I help you?'

'I'd like to speak to Mr Myles please.'

'Who is calling?'

'This is David Cole.'

'What do you wish to speak to Mr Myles about?'

'A personal matter.'

He could hear the secretary draw breath before coming out with some practised polite refusal and so he quickly added: 'It's about the casting of Kate Barlow in the part of Irene in 'The Spider Trap'. I'm her agent.'

Another pause and then: 'Just one moment.'

There was silence on the line for about a minute then a dark brown voice spoke.

'Julian Myles.'

'It's about Kate.'

'Yes. Who is this exactly?'

'David, David Cole.'

'Oh yes, I do believe I remember Kate mentioning you. Are you acting as her agent now?'

'No, not really. I'd just like you to tell me about last night.' As soon as he said it, David knew it sounded like a ridiculous challenge of some jealous boyfriend.

'Last night? I'm afraid I'm not with you.'

David felt a chill of concern. 'You had dinner with Kate last night to discuss a part in 'The Spider Trap'.'

'You've got it wrong, I'm afraid.' Julian Myles now sounded irritable. 'I was busy all last night, shooting. I've not seen Kate in ages. She did ring me yesterday to say she was interested in the part and I said I'd get back to her later in the week; but I didn't see her last night.'

David was stunned. He managed to mumble some apology and end the call as quickly as he could. What did this mean? Myles' voice had all the irritation and veracity of truth; and anyway, there was no reason for him to lie. Therefore, it was Kate who had lied. In God's name, why? And what was more important: where the hell had she been last night?

* * *

'This is most irregular,' said Mrs Drabble, peering over her half-rimmed glasses.

Rob Moore gave his broadest grin. 'Ah, but television is a most irregular medium,' he said charmingly, bending towards her.

She pulled back quickly and stood up. 'Well, I will inform the headmaster of your request. If you will take a seat.'

'Certainly.' The teeth flashed again.

Mrs Drabble scurried out of the room while Rob sat back in a chair. He felt relaxed and at ease. He was enjoying playing the role.

He was enjoying life.

He glanced around the tidy but quaint office. The mellowed woodwork, the antiquated typewriter, the faded Stubbs reproduction, hanging slightly askew it was all redolent of the desperate attempt to create an image. The world of a bygone age held together by a shoestring. And with these fading standards came the arrogance and suspicion such as he had met with Mrs Drabble, the headmaster's secretary—such as he felt sure he would meet in Brett, the headmaster. But his smile would win the day. He knew it.

At length Mrs Drabble returned. 'The headmaster will see you now.'

'Thank you, dear lady. It was a pleasure to meet you.' He beamed and gave a little bow. Mrs Drabble was non-plussed.

Rob tapped lightly at the headmaster's door and entered. A frosty middle-aged man looked up from his desk as he did so.

'Mr Brett, how nice to meet you again.' Rob thrust forward his hand an expansive greeting.

'I was not aware that we had met before,' said the head tentatively as his hand was grasped in a hearty shake.

'Oh yes, one of young Timothy's sports days. A splendid occasion. A credit to the school and you in particular.'

'Thank you.' The frost showed no signs of melting.

Rob gazed around the room. 'This is an excellent place. Believe me, I do not flatter. I was impressed before, but today seeing some of your classes and really drinking in the atmosphere—well, as I say, excellent! I am certainly keen to send my boy here.'

'Oh really. How old?'

'Ah, romper stage yet. But they grow so quickly, don't they?' Another smooth grin.

'Indeed they do.' A thaw appeared to be setting in.

'Now then about young Timothy...' The head's expression changed, the forehead puckering.

'Has your secretary explained the situation?' continued Rob.

'Not in detail, Mr Moore.'

'Please call me Rob. Well I'm a close friend of Timothy's mother, Kate Barlow—the actress y'know?'

The head nodded.

'At Paragon Productions we're doing a programme called 'Off-springs', a sort of sociological documentary where we interview parents whose professional life puts them in the public eye—politicians, sports people, writers, actors and so on. We also interview the children to see how they perceive their parents and how public pressure affects their relationship. It's a very interesting project.'

The head remained silent, but nodded, almost imperceptibly.

'So I want to borrow Timothy for the day to do the recording.'

The head pursed his lips. 'This is most irregular,' he said echoing the secretary's words as though they were both carrying out some verbal ritual to repel any disturbance to the quiet orderly routine of the school.

'I am aware of that, headmaster, and we've no wish to disrupt Timothy's education more than absolutely necessary. Surely one day cannot make all that difference? And of course it will give Mrs Barlow a chance to see her son. She has been missing him badly since her husband died. It was only her consideration for the continuity of Timothy's schooling that prevented her from moving him to a day school near her home.' He paused to allow the implication of his words to sink in.

'I don't wish to be awkward Mr Moore,' the head replied with no trace of conciliation in his voice, 'but we do stipulate in our rules that the school requires parents to give us twenty four hours' notice before they remove their son away—except in emergencies of course.'

'I fully appreciate that, but unfortunately the world of television works on the 'now' principle and we often do not have the luxury of advance notice. If we don't do the recording today, we may have missed the boat. In a sense, I suppose you could say it was an emergency.' He leaned forward, smiling. 'And, of course, Mr Brett, you can be assured that St. Austell's will be given full credit in the programme. Quite a nice little plug for the school.'

The idea of St. Austell's being 'plugged' in a television programme did not appeal to the headmaster at all, but the thought of its possible effect—increased subscription and therefore higher revenue—did. He pondered a moment, basking in the warmth of Rob's smile, before replying.

'I take it that Mrs Barlow is in full agreement with this?'

'Of course. I thought I had made myself clear on that matter.' The sun quickly set on Rob's demeanour. 'I have a letter here from her, if you don't wish to take my word on the matter.' He fumbled with dramatic irritation in his jacket pocket.

'No, no, Mr Moore, that will not be necessary. I was in no way suggesting that what you have told me is untrue; but you will appreciate that I have to get my facts correct, if I am to release a boy from my care.'

The smile returned. Of course.'

'Good. Then if you will wait a moment I will have Timothy brought here.'

'That is extremely kind of you.'

***

David sat thoughtfully staring out to sea. If Kate had lied to him about where she was going last night, how many other lies had she told him? All that stuff about starting fresh over again. The claim that she loved him. It couldn't all be lies. He knew that, deep down.

He tried to face the situation rationally. He knew for certain that she had decided to take the part in that thriller as she had told him. That was true; Myles confirmed that. Therefore something must have happened yesterday—something unexpected. Something that compelled her to go somewhere last night—a place she didn't want him to know about so she had made up this story about having dinner with the director. It was a story she thought would never be checked.

So what had happened yesterday? Surely not another Michael experience. He stiffened as he remembered how he'd found her on Friday night. He clenched his fist. Not that. Please. He could contend with most things but not the ghost of a dead husband.

Come on, come on, he told himself. Let's be more positive. He began pacing the floor, his mind searching for Kate's subterfuge. Perhaps she was planning some surprise for him?

Maybe she went to see Timothy. A sudden urge to see her son? That was understandable. She'd never been completely happy with him at St. Austell's and after Michael's death she had been tempted to remove him. It was the thought of disrupting his education that had prevented her; that, and the awareness of her own mental instability. Now perhaps she had decided to bring him home to be part of her new start in life. Maybe that was it.

As much as he tried to accept this theory, David was not convinced. She would hardly have felt that need to lie to me over that. He turned and faced the room and then his eyes lit upon the black plastic bag the hospital had given him containing Kate's belongings. Perhaps there was a solution to the mystery in there.

***

'Hello, Tim, old chap.' Rob Moore held out his hand.

Timothy Barlow took it automatically, surprised by the coldness. The faint trace of bewilderment in his eyes did not go unnoticed by the headmaster.

'You know who this gentleman is, don't you, Timothy?'

The boy nodded. 'A friend of my mother's—Mr Moore.'

'Rob. You can call me Rob.' The teeth blazed.

Inside the shell of Rob Moore, the entity that was Michael Barlow pulsated with emotion. It longed to take the boy in his arms, his son, envelop him—to keep him for his own. But the controlling mind kept all these emotions in check. The dark waters swirled, but all was calm on the surface.

The control was perfect. After all, the mind thought, the boy was only a pawn after all, only a pawn.

***

David rummaged through Kate's belongings. There was nothing here. Just elements of Kate. He fingered her delicate underwear, not for any erotic thrill but for the sensation of gentleness and nearness.

He left her handbag until last.

He opened it and picked his way through the contents. Nothing unusual; all very predictable. Then he noticed the card. Bent in two at the bottom of the bag was a dog-eared white card: a visiting card by the look of it. David pulled it out and examined it.

On the back there was a roughly drawn map, an address, a date - yesterday's - and the time 8.30. scribbled in pencil. On the front in italicised print, David read:

Arthur Crabtree
Medium & Clairvoyant
Reasonable Rates

NINE

Mrs Hardwicke was late. Unusually late. She was cross with herself because of it. She prided herself on her reliability and being punctual was the main aspect of this. She hated being late and it wasn't just because Mrs Moore wasn't as easy going as some of her clients; it was a personal thing with her.

However, as she struggled down the driveway with her bag, she was surprised to see that the downstairs curtains were still drawn. She'd never known that before. Perhaps she wasn't the only one who was behind with themselves this morning. She gave the bell her usual three rings and entered.

The door was unlocked. Not even Mr M, drunk as he had been at times, had ever left the door unlocked before going to bed. Still, Mrs Hardwicke mused, there was always a first time.

It was gloomy and dark in the hall—and still. Very still. Instinctively she felt there was something not quite right and her skin began to ripple with goose pimples.

'Hello,' she called out. 'Mrs M?'

Her voice was swallowed up in the unnatural silence. Surely she can't still be in bed? Hubby was always out of the house by this time—off to his job at that TV place. She hardly ever saw him. She was glad of that. She liked Mrs M—but really didn't care for her hubby. She couldn't quite say why—it was just a feeling rather than a reason.

Mrs Hardwicke felt no inclination to take her coat off and get on with the job of cleaning—not until she knew what was going on. She wandered into the kitchen. It was tidy and clean. No breakfast had been prepared in here today. Maybe she was still in bed then. She glanced at the clock on the wall, coming up to eleven. Surely not at this time?

With little enthusiasm and less volume than before, she called out again. There was no reply. Nothing.

She moved from the kitchen, back into the hall and into the sitting room. Something made her shudder as she crossed the threshold; the skin tingled at the back of her neck.

And then she saw it: the head of her employer—pale, rigid and ghastly, staring at her from the carpet. It was some moments before Mrs Hardwicke came to realise what she was seeing. And when she did, she was too terrified to scream.

***

The words on the tatty little card resounded in David's head: Medium and Clairvoyant. They meant only one thing: contact with the dead. Not that the dead could be contacted, only in some theatrical sideshow with disembodied heads, spirit voices and similar jiggery-pokery. It was the world of glass diamonds and pinchbeck gold watches. And Kate had been to visit one of these charlatans. For what reason. The answer was obvious. To contact Michael, of course. To contact her dead husband.

The whole thing would be laughable if it weren't so bloody tragic. Fucking tragic. He gained some mild sense of comfort from the obscenity.

Why had she been so stupid? Was her need to contact Michael so great that it squeezed all logic out of her? Despite all she had said to him about putting the past behind her, it must have been that her guilt, her conscience—call it what you will—had over-ridden all other considerations. So she had lied to him and gone seeking her dead husband to say she was sorry.

Jesus Christ!

David's hand gripped the steering wheel as the anger swelled up inside him. He glanced at the speedometer and saw that the little white arm was sweeping past the accepted speed limit for the road. Slowly he eased off the accelerator. There was nothing to be gained by behaving stupidly. Whatever Kate did—she had done it. Nothing he did could change that fact. All he could do now was to find out what actually happened at this Arthur Crabtree's place last night. What tricks had been played on her.

What farcical messages from the grave had been elicited to comfort the grieving widow? David roared with anger at the thought. It was quite obvious to him that whatever had occurred at this blasted medium's house it had caused Kate some emotional upset that had caused her to drive erratically and crash.

David felt his anger increase. His face muscles stiffened and his teeth clenched. Even in death, Michael was still hurting them. Of course there had been no real message from Michael— probably just a pre-recorded tape sufficiently distorted to sound ethereal and characterless. If not that some equally devious fraudulent device which had manufactured the spirit voice. It was Kate's susceptibility and her feelings of guilt that had graced it with reality. Reality. Hah! That was a choice word. A very choice word.

He ran through the scenario in his mind: the voice of Michael, 'Darling, I'll always love you'—Kate receiving no reply to her pleas for forgiveness, absolution, release—just the repeated message, 'Darling, I love you.' He could see her hurrying out into the night, crying, upset, wretched, still carrying her burden of guilt. She would drive away emotionally high, tears blinding her eyes, her mind in turmoil. Failing to see the road clearly, she swerves, skids... and crashes.

And now she lies in Intensive Care, on the brink of death. All because of bloody Michael. And this Arthur Crabtree.

David pulled over to the side of the road and jumped out. As though he were choking, he gulped in the sweet cold air, his whole body shaking with emotion. Leaning on the roof of the car he laid his head on his arms. It was as though over the years he had built a solid wall—a dam wall—to protect his life from tears, pain and involvement and now the dam had burst flooding him with all these unfamiliar painful sensations. Some small thought grew in his mind. Really, he was the one to blame for this. For all this. If only he had been more supportive, more open, more willing to express his emotions, his love for Kate, maybe she would not have needed to allow Michael to dominate her life, even after he had died.

He breathed deeply. I will never let her down again, he vowed. Just let her live.

He stayed like immobile for some minutes allowing these thoughts to settle in his mind and then got back into the car. He lit a cigarette and inhaled deeply. God, that was good. He felt his inner rhythm settling and a calmer mood evolving. He leaned back, his eyes closed, enjoying the smoke, letting his mind go blank. Finally, he stubbed the cigarette out and picked up the card from the dashboard. He examined the crudely drawn map, fixing the directions in his mind once more. Right, let's see what this Arthur Crabtree has to say for himself.

***

Tim sat quietly in the passenger seat as the barren hedgerows flashed by in a dark blur. He had spoken but a few words to Rob Moore since they had left the headmaster's study. He was pleased to be leaving St. Austell's even if it was only for a day and delighted at the prospect of seeing his mother again, but he felt uneasy with this man. There was something about him that Tim sensed was not quite right. In one way he seemed very familiar and yet there was something cold and alien about him.

Tim surreptitiously turned and glanced at him. He was sitting erect, looking directly ahead at the road. His movements were stiff and mechanical—like a robot. The face registered no emotion, except the eyes and they were bright and glittering and, thought Tim, did not, in some crazy way, go with the face.

The warmth of the heater and the easy steady motion of the car made him feel drowsy. This was understandable: he had slept badly the night before and was very tired. But somehow, he didn't want to fall asleep. Not in the presence of this man.

Instinctively, he did not feel safe.

He blinked his eyes rapidly as though to shake off the heavy weight which was pressing down on his eyelids. He shifted his position in the seat in order to make himself less comfortable. His movement caught the attention of Rob Moore and he turned to look at the boy. The face was immobile, motionless, almost like the face of a...Tim's mind searched for a suitable comparison, a simile as his English teacher would have said. A face like a... like a waxwork figure. He remembered being taken by his mother to the Chamber of Horrors at Madame Tussauds in London. He was thrilled and a little bit frightened by those gruesome mannequins. Here was one come to life. Only the eyes were real and they glittered darkly at him. He could not avoid their gaze—their hypnotic gaze.

He began to feel very strange indeed. The weights were even heavier on his eyelids now. He was losing the battle to keep awake; and the noise of the car engine began to fade away as though someone was controlling a volume switch.

Tim fought the overwhelming tiredness he felt but inexorably the eyelids began flicker downwards. Turning to Rob Moore again, it seemed to him now as though he were looking down a long tunnel at his face. The eyes appeared to have changed: they were without pupils now and completely black—a shiny viscous black, like a rippling oil slick.

As his own lids closed, shutting out the real world, Tim did not sink into sleep. He thought not anyway. He just felt as though he had been transferred to a dark, silent world. A soft velvet almost tangible blackness enveloped him. However, he didn't feel frightened; on the contrary he felt very relaxed.

Little specks of light like stars flickered across his vision and then one star remained, growing brighter, larger. It wasn't a pure brightness for there were shadows on its surface—distinguishable shadows. As it grew, getting nearer to Tim or at least as it seemed to get nearer to him because in that black void, distance could not be judged, the star revealed itself to be a face.

It was the face of Rob Moore. The dead pan face with the glittery eyes.

And then something strange happened to the face. The features rippled and as though the waxwork figure had come too close to the heat, the face began to melt and then blend, forming another face. A more familiar face.

The face of his father.

'Hello, Timothy,' the face said, in the rough familiar tones the boy knew.

'Dad,' he heard himself, say while realising that he had not actually spoken.

'You see, I was good as my word. I said that I would come back.'

'But... you can't come back. You're...' He didn't want to use that word. Dead.

'Here I am. I have come back. Trust me. I am your father. You are my flesh and blood—part of me. And I live again. I have come back for you and your mother. You are both mine.'

There was no warmth in this statement and Tim felt no joy in hearing it. In this weird dream-state where reality had no place, he still could not believe what he had been told. He knew his father was dead.

The face before him smiled and the eyes twinkled.

'Everything is fine, Tim. There will be no further upset. I'm back to stay. I'm back to look after you.'

This time the voice seemed to penetrate deeper into Tim's brain, feeling its way along the winding convolutions, soothing and numbing as it went. A warmth filtered through Tim, relaxing him and easing away reason. There was no pressure any more. He believed. He believed his father. Gently and serenely he succumbed to the illusion and just before he sank happily into the darkness once more, the thoughts were seeded in his mind.

The car pulled up sharply at some traffic lights. Tim was jerked forward and awoke.

'Sorry about that,' said Rob Moore. 'I didn't expect them to change so quickly.' He turned and smiled at the boy.

Timothy smiled back and replied, dreamily: 'That's all right, Dad.'

***

David sat in his car looking at Crabtree's house. It looked like an ordinary house in an ordinary street. Both the street and house looked dingy and run-down—but ordinary. The green door with peeling paint appeared innocent and bland. It was here that Kate came last night in search of her dead husband.

What travesties had taken place inside that shabby dwelling David could only guess and he wouldn't trust his imagination that far: he wanted to know the truth.

Slowly and purposefully, he got out of the car, locked it and approached the house. After a split second's hesitation, he knocked. The noise resounded hollowly down the hall fading into the house.

There was no response.

He knocked again: harder and longer.

A cold breeze blew down the deserted street stirring up shreds of litter in the gutter. Only faintly could he hear the traffic from a nearby road—the real world. It seemed distant and alien here.

Again, there was no response to his knock. He looked in at the grime-streaked windows, but the curtains were drawn. At this time of day? It was after one. He was growing angry now. He wasn't going away until he knew all about last night.

He flipped open the letter box and peered into the murky hallway. There was no sign of life. He called out through the open flap, his voice ringing against the bare walls. In angry frustration he grasped the door handle and turned it violently. To his surprise the door swung open. It hadn't been locked.

He walked in quickly, closing the door behind him and found that he was standing on a litter of morning mail. Perhaps Crabtree was still in bed. David picked up one of the letters and examined the envelope. This was the right address, all right— the same one that had been on the card he'd found in Kate's handbag.

Dropping the letter to the floor, he ventured further into the house. There was something about the place that upset him. Was it the unnatural silence, the gloom of the place, or the smell. Yes, it was the smell. It was an all-pervading aroma. He couldn't attach a name to it; he only knew it turned his stomach.

As he pushed open the door of the sitting room, a strange sight met his eyes. This was the room at the front of the house with its curtains drawn. The only illumination was the meagre fire struggling for its life in the grate. In an armchair by the fire, sitting bolt upright was a pale faced little man. A mousey middle-aged woman sat hunched up at his feet, her head on his lap. She was murmuring something to the man, but David could not make out the words.

At the sound of his entrance, the woman slowly lifted her head and looked at him. However there was no surprise in her dull eyes which surveyed him through this pebble glasses.

'Hello,' she said, with a child-like lilt in her voice. 'It's so nice of you to come.'

'Mrs Crabtree?'

The woman hesitated slightly before replying. 'Yes, that's right. I'm Mrs Crabtree, and this,' she turned to the little man, 'is Arthur. Mr Crabtree, my husband. Say hello, Arthur.'

David came a few steps forward and then stopped abruptly. Looking at the chalk-white face of Arthur Crabtree, grotesquely animated by the flickering flames, he could see from the vacant gorgon stare and the slack gaping mouth that the man was dead. He grasped the podgy hand. It had the chill of dead meat. He felt for a pulse. There was none.

David found himself stating the obvious. 'He's dead'.

The woman just smiled. 'Oh no, sir. No. You've got that wrong. He's just resting. He'll be all right after he's had his little nap. Won't you Arthur dear?' She kissed the dead man's fingers.

David shook his head in disbelief. This was like a scene from some suburban bedlam. The woman was obviously mentally unbalanced. Whether this was as a result of the man's death or not he didn't know, but at the present moment he was aware that there was no point in trying to reason with her.

'Just resting. He'll be his old self soon; you'll see, sir. Won't you, Arthur?' The pale white face with the dead eyes stared blankly back at her.

The woman then turned, smiling, to David. 'He deserves his rest. He's had a tiring night, but it was worth it. He made contact again; real contact.'

'Contact?' said David, his pulse quickening.

'With the other side. With those who have passed over.'

'Who did he contact?' asked David more brusquely than he intended.

'Arthur will be alright after his little nap, you'll see.'

'Who did Arthur contact last night?'

The woman looked blankly at him.

'Was it Michael Barlow? Mrs Barlow's husband? I know she had an appointment here at seven thirty last night.'

At the mention of Kate's name, the woman's features clouded. 'Mrs Barlow,' she repeated slowly as if resurrecting a fragment from her long forgotten past.

'Yes. Yes. Mrs Barlow,' David urged. 'She was here last night.' The woman nodded. David felt his stomach turn. He had been right then. But oh he wished he hadn't.

The woman shivered. Memories she hoped she'd buried flickered into her brain returned to her. 'Cold,' she said. 'I'm cold.' She threw her arms around herself and began to rock gently backwards and forwards.

'Yes, it is a little chilly. I'll put some more coal on the fire for you,' said David, humouring her. He had to get some sense out of the woman if he could. There would be no help forthcoming from Arthur Crabtree.

Yellow tongues of fire flared up as he emptied a shovel of coal into the grate. Grotesque shadows leapt around the room as though in response to the renewed vigour of the fire.

'Is that better?'

The woman nodded mutely and gave David a timid smile.

'Now then, will you tell me what happened here last night?' The woman's face turned sour again and she turned away from him.

'Please tell me, Mrs Crabtree. I've got to know.' He knelt down by her and took her hand.

She gazed up at him and a gentle smile touched her lips. 'It was to be an important meeting. You see Arthur had really made contact. There was no fooling this time: he really had made contact. He was so excited that after all these years his power had come back to him.'

'Who did he make contact with?'

She seemed not to have heard David's urgent plea and carried on talking as though he hadn't spoken. She was really talking to herself.

'He was worried, too. Arthur was. The contact was very powerful and he thought it might be too strong for him to handle. But he couldn't deny its request you see.' She smiled again as she gazed down into the fire. 'He needed to prove to himself that he could still do it. After all these years of faking it and pretending, here was a chance to show that he could do it for real. The Power had come back to him. But he was worried. He didn't say as much, but I knew, a wife can always tell. She knows these things.'

She dropped her head on her chest and lapsed into silence. David waited a few moments before prompting her.

'Tell me what happened?'

She heard these words faintly as they broke through the confusion of her own thoughts. 'What happened? Arthur made contact. He made contact with the woman's husband.'

David suddenly felt nauseous and found he could hardly breathe. God, I wish I could wake up, he told himself. This is all a bad dream. He did not want to believe what he was hearing. But he did. Crabtree had contacted Michael Barlow from beyond the grave and now Crabtree was dead and Kate was in Intensive Care. It was a fucking living nightmare. And then he remembered what Rob Moore had said the day before: 'My waking moments are like a dream and those damned nightmares are the reality.' It seemed that he too had been sucked into this dark realm.

Rather more roughly than he intended, he grasped the woman by the shoulders and shook her. 'Tell me exactly what went on here last night.'

She did not seem to notice his harshness and replied softly to his demand. 'I told you Arthur made contact.'

With Michael Barlow, Mrs Barlow's husband?'

Her eyes widened. 'Yes, that's right.'

'What did he say?'

'Say?'

'Yes, what was his message?'

'He said he wanted... Life. That's all. He wanted Life.'

Jesus Christ. 'What else did he say? He must have said more.'

She turned away from him to face the fire. 'He didn't say anything else—he just …came back.'

'Came back,' he reiterated, not daring to comprehend what she meant. Those two simple everyday words had the Devil's curse on them.

'Arthur opened the channel for him to return, you see.' As she spoke these words, it was as though she was reminded again how it had really been—the hideous truth that she had pushed into the farthest corner of her mind, hoping to forget about it for ever. She threw herself into the dead man's lap and sobbed. 'No. No. Arthur dear.' Her voice trailed away into a tearful whisper.

Struggling to make sense of this crazy woman's words, David realised that the situation was far blacker than he could fully comprehend. Although her story presented an impossible scenario ripped from the page of a horror novel, the facts contrived to support this surreal fantasy. However, his logic rebelled against such nonsense. He might allow for the possibility of spirit messages, telepathic contact of some kind with the bereaved which provided the 'medium' with a rich source of data from which he could concoct a convincing message from the other side. But dead men did not come back to life. They did not walk again.

He looked at the pallid face of Arthur Crabtree. It was obvious that the séance had been too much for him. Kate was clearly too intelligent a woman to be easily fooled and he'd had to pull out all the stops to present a convincing performance. The strain had been too much and he must have suffered some kind of heart attack.

It was as simple as that. Wasn't it? WASN'T IT?

And of course Crabtree's sudden death is what upset Kate. Not some daft message from Michael. It was the shock of Crabtree's demise that had caused Kate to drive so erratically.

David almost smiled with relief as the clear rational explanation of events formed in his mind, expelling all macabre thoughts of walking corpses and such like.

'Look Mrs Crabtree, will you allow me to ring for a doctor? I do think your husband should be seen to,' he said as gently as he could, putting his hand on her shoulder.

She turned her tear-stained face to David. Her eyes seemed to have lost that remote quality; the mistiness and the faraway look had disappeared. Her features were now relaxed and a slight smile touched her lips.

'I'm all right now. It's all been a bit of a shock, you understand, but I assure you that I'm perfectly all right now. I loved him so much, you see. It's painful to lose one you love, you know.'

David knew.

'You've been very kind,' she continued, 'but I would prefer to ring the doctor myself. He is my husband.'

'Of course.'

'If you'll leave me now, I'd like to spend a few minutes alone with him before I ring. A few last private moments together.'

David knew there was no point in opposing her on this. There was nothing further he could do here, so he may as well leave. He had at least put the missing pieces of the puzzle together and although the completed picture was far from pleasant, at least now he knew.

'I'll leave you in peace then,' he replied gently, getting up.

As he reached the door, he turned back and said, 'I'm sorry.'

But the woman did not really hear him; she was staring into the dead face of the man she loved. Closing the door on this pathetic tableau, David left the house.

After some moments, Jean Wilson spoke. 'You're cold, Arthur. Very cold. So am I, my dear. We could do with some more warmth. I think I'd better build a bigger fire, eh?'

Although Arthur Crabtree did not reply, she knew that he agreed with her.

She emptied the contents of the magazine rack onto the coals and began to stuff anything flammable into the grate, piling up fuel around the hearth. The flames blazed, crackled and stretched. Sparks became airborne, landing on the rug. Jean Wilson seemed oblivious of the growing conflagration or the spark that landed on the hem of her long floral dress. She remained immobile, sitting at Crabtree's feet, her eyes shining in the glare of the flames.

TEN

The letter 't' in Vista had somehow gone missing and the sign now read. Vis a Hotel'. That little idiosyncrasy fell in with the rest of the hotel's appearance: it looked all right, but there seemed to be something missing.

Fragments of Rob Moore' memory still clung to the mind that now inhabited the body and it was these that faintly remembered the hotel, conveying the information to the new brain. Something to do with bringing a secretary here for an illicit night of passion. A smile crossed Rob's features. The memory was useful. It did suggest that the hotel was used to shady customers involved in a no-questions-asked room booking and that was ideal. Just what he wanted.

It was a grey day; looking out to sea it was difficult to determine where the sky met the water. The promenade in this unfashionable end of Brighton was deserted. It was like Doomsday.

'Just wait here, Timothy,' he said. 'I won't be long.'

'Yes,' the boy said mechanically.

Rob Moore got out of the car, shivered as the winter cold hit him, and crossed the road to the hotel.

The reception hall was quite smart with a plastic potted palm, but there was in the air the aroma of over-cooked vegetables that permeate such establishments.

The girl at the desk, young, heavily made-up, bored, was reading a magazine. At Rob's approach she looked up, without interest, and said nothing.

'I'd like a room for the night.'

It took some time for the girl to respond as though the request had been difficult to comprehend. 'Single or double,' she said at last in a flat monotone.

'Double. It's for myself and my son.'

The girl registered a flicker of interest.

'Oh yeah,' she said, the words hardly concealing her interpretation of the situation. 'With or without ensuite facilities?'

'With.'

'How long for?'

'I'm not sure. One or maybe two nights.'

'We'll need to credit card for security.'

Rob did not have a credit card. Something he had not reckoned on. He had secured quite a stash of money from the house, but he'd not thought of a credit card.

'I'll pay cash for tonight,' he said as fumbled with his wallet.

'That'll be seventy five pounds,' the girl said.

He counted out the notes and handed them over.

'Sign the book. Regulations,' she said, revealing a tatty register under her magazine. He scrawled a name in the book and then she gave him a key with a large rectangle of orange plastic attached.

'Room 3B. Second floor at the front.'

'Thank you. I'll just go and get my son from the car.'

After he had gone, the girl mouthed the word 'Pervert'—then, before resuming her reading she glanced at the signature in the register.

It read: 'Michael Barlow'.

***

The road was blurred. Headlights were merging into one amorphous brightness that seemed to engulf her. She struggled with the wheel, wrenching it from one side to the other, wildly trying to control the car. All her efforts were to no avail. The car seemed to be travelling on a pre-ordained path and nothing she could do would alter its course. The noise of blaring horns and screeching brakes filled her ears as she saw through the rain-lashed windscreen a hedge coming towards her.

And then there was blackness.

The dark was almost welcoming. As it guarded her, she seemed to lose all sense of feeling. For moments she was numb. Then came the pain; the searing, agonising pain. Where did it hurt most? She couldn't tell: it was all over.

Then mercifully, it went. It was as though the word pain had been chalked in large letters on a blackboard and some unseen hand had wiped it clean.

Now she was in a white world—a snowscape dotted here and there with brightly coloured carousels which whirled as the delicate snowflakes decorated the air. She stood by one carousel watching the painted horses prance by, captivated by their flowing yellow manes, wild staring eyes and flashing black hooves. Up and down, up and down they went. How she longed to be with them, to spin round in the frosty air, but every horse had a rider, each wearing a shiny coloured mask with broad painted smiles on them.

Gently the carousel began to slow down. The horses' prancing grew less frantic, moving from gallop to a canter to a trot. And then they stopped.

The giant whirligig shuddered to a silent halt but no one made a move to get off. The riders sat motionless, clinging to the chromium poles, their painted faces staring down at her. It was as though they were saying, 'Sorry, lady, you can't join us. It is not allowed.'

She ran through the snow that lay all around the carousel in search of a horse that was free. She must ride—she must. And then she saw one; it must have been there all the time, but she hadn't noticed it.

The carousel attendant came across and beckoned her aboard. He held out his hand to help her on. She took it and stepped on to the carousel. Turning to thank the attendant, she saw that he too was wearing a painted mask.

Suddenly the carousel jerked into motion and the attendant pointed urgently to the empty mount. The ride started again. Quickly she clambered astride the horse just as it began to move upwards. She felt the cold air brush against her face as the carousel began to pick up speed. Snowflakes swept past her face, leaving for a brief moment tiny sensations of cold.

Up and down.

Faster and faster.

Up and down.

Soon she was flying with the world a white blur, splashed occasionally with streaks of colour. She felt exhilarated and yet, at the same time strangely frightened.

She looked round her fellow riders, and saw that one by one they were taking off their masks. To her surprise, she saw that underneath they had blank faces: there were no features, just smooth pale skin. She shuddered and turned away. I don't like this, I want to get off, she told herself. She gripped the silver pole tighter and wished the carousel would stop.

Gradually, the horses began to slow down. They moved from a gallop, to a canter, to a trot and then with a sudden jolt, they stopped altogether. The attendant stepped forward and helped her down and as he did so, he pulled off his mask as well. But he was not like the rest: he did not have a pale featureless face. He had the rotting decaying features of a corpse. Maggots squirmed in the eye sockets and wriggled out of the mouth. He moved closer, his arms outstretched ready to embrace her.

The nurse on duty ran quickly to the bed when she heard the patient crying out. She was calling a man's name.

***

By the time the fire brigade arrived, long yellow tongues of fire were busily devouring the front of the house. The green paint of the front door had shrivelled and blackened before surrendering to the flames.

The officer in charge of operations stood back from the heat and shook his head. 'Whoever is in that lot is a goner. There's no way we can go in. All we can do is stop it from spreading—with a bit of luck.'

The usually empty street was thronged with the curious. Pale impassive faces stared at the fire as if mesmerised by the colour and heat of the flames.

Inside the house, at the heart of the inferno, two still bodies were roasting, charring and fusing into each other.

***

'There has been some improvement, Mr Cole.' The Scottish nurse gave him a reassuring smile.

'Yes?'

'Nothing very dramatic, mind you, but she has used her voice. She called out something earlier. That shows she's fighting her way to consciousness.'

David felt a warm thrill of pleasure.

'And that's good.' It was half question and half self-assurance.

'Yes. It shows that she wants to survive and, in these cases, that can mean much more than any help we can give.'

David nodded. 'Thank you,' he said, managing a ghost of a smile.

The nurse turned to leave but he stopped her with a gesture.

'You say that she called out something. What exactly did she say?'

'It was someone's name. A man's name,' she puzzled for a moment. 'Oh yes, that's it. She called out the name Michael.'

***

Rob Moore pulled down the blind in the dingy room. Dull though it was, the light was beginning to hurt his eyes. He needed a rest. The body felt heavy and tired. He glanced over at Tim who was lying on the single bed watching him.

'What happens now, Dad?' said the boy slowly, dully.

'We rest.' He moved closer to the boy and placed a hand on his forehead. 'Just relax, Timothy, and rest. Rest.' The boy's body visibly went limp and although his eyes remained open, they were glazed and vacant. 'Good boy.'

Rob Moore laid down on his own bed, his hands behind his head. Time for him to rest, too. Soon it would be dark and then it would be time for a change. It would be too dangerous for him to maintain the Rob Moore shell any longer; and besides he needed a new body for the next stage of his plan.

A stranger, this time.

Someone David Cole did not know
***

David was exhausted. He felt as though he were carrying the weight of the world on his shoulders. It had been the worst day of his life and he wanted to sleep for a while, to get some temporary rest—to escape from the mess. He didn't want to think about what had happened or what might happen in the future. All he wanted was to soak a while in a hot bath, have a good sleep and then he might be able to face the world again. He knew that he really should get in touch with Tim's school and let the boy know of his mother's accident. He had a right to know, but David couldn't face that particular drama just now. And anyway, it would only freak the boy out to see his mother in such a state. He just needed a rest for a few hours and then it would be time for him to visit the hospital anyway.

However, his plans were not to be realised for he had only just started running the bath when the doorbell rang. Wearily he plodded to the front door and for the second time in twenty-four hours he was confronted by a policeman on his doorstep. In this instance there were two of them and they were plain clothes officers, but David could see beyond them into the drive and saw their saloon and a white police car behind it. They had obviously come in convoy.

What now? David thought. What the hell now? Pray God it isn't bad news about Kate.

'Mr Cole?'

He nodded. 'We are police officers.' The shorter of the two flashed a card. 'May we come in?'

David stepped back and gestured them to enter. He led them into the sitting room and then without speaking, turned to face them. 'It's about Rob Moore, a close colleague of yours.'

David nodded. 'Rob. Yes. A friend also,' he said, non-plussed, suddenly seized by a sense of dread. 'What about him?'

'Do you know where he is?'

David frowned and ran his fingers through his hair. What the hell was this all about? 'Well, not at this moment. I presume you've tried his home and the office at Paragon...'

'He's not been there today,' said the taller detective, as though reading from a notebook.

'And neither have you,' observed the other pointedly.

'No, my—girlfriend has been in a car accident. She's in Intensive Care. I've just come back from seeing her.' He moved his arms in some kind of inarticulate gesture. His tired brain was too sluggish for him to be eloquent. The two detectives looked non-committal and said nothing. There were no signs of understanding or sympathy in their stern expression. 'So what has Rob done that warrants a posse?'

Neither man smiled. The shorter of the two, obviously the superior officer, looked seriously at David through his gold-rimmed glasses.

'I'm afraid this is not a light-hearted matter, Mr Cole. We are investigating a murder.'

'Rob's been murdered?' David realised the foolishness of this remark as soon as he'd uttered it. If Rob was dead, Holmes and Watson here would hardly be looking for him. However, the other alternative was also incredible.

'No sir, Mr Moore has not been murdered, but we have reason to believe he may be involved in a killing.'

David began to feel the now familiar sensation of unease gnawing in the pit of his stomach. 'Who... who is dead?'

'Mrs Moore.'

'Fiona?'

Both men nodded.

David went cold and his stomach burned. 'I don't... I don't understand.' He shook his head in disbelief and slumped into a chair. What was happening to his life? What maniac was writing this script?

'Mrs Moore was found by a cleaner this morning. She had been brutally murdered. There was no sign of a break in or of Mr Moore; and therefore, we are anxious to contact him regarding this affair.'

What farcical language they use, thought David. It was the most pretentious euphemism he'd ever heard. The truth was that they thought Rob had killed his wife, done a bunk and now they were after him.

'I'm sorry, I can't help you.' He paused and changed the phrasing. 'I'm not able to help you. I don't know where he is.'

'Did he have any private haunts he liked to visit?'

Haunts? There was a phrase. David shook his head.

'How had he been acting in the last few days? Did his behaviour seem odd in any way?'

Yes, thought David. Bloody odd. He was haunted by a dead man and the last time I saw him he was like a walking zombie. But that proved nothing.

'Not that I noticed.' he said.

'What about his wife? Did they get on?'

David could not help giving a brittle smile. 'They tolerated each other. I wouldn't say it was a happy marriage, but they each did their own thing and it worked.'

'What was Rob's thing?' asked the junior officer. 'Other women?'

'Not recently. Or at least not that I know of.'

'Would he be likely to confide in you about them?' asked gold rims.

David shrugged his shoulders. 'He has occasionally in the past.'

'When was the last time?'

'Oh, God, I don't know. A long time ago now. Over a year. Look these weren't great passions. He'd just take some little starry-eyed secretary out for a meal and a quick bang in the back of his car. There were no romantic entanglements. It was just for sex.' David hated himself as soon as he'd said that, despite it being the truth.

'What about his wife? What were their sexual relationship like?'

'From what I could gather she was a little cool.'

'Frigid?'

'A little cool. Look, I only worked with the man; didn't sit at the end of his bed taking notes.' The two detectives ignored the last remark.

'I know one thing: Rob was not a violent man. I can't believe he would... kill anyone. Let alone his own wife.'

The two policemen seemed to disregard this remark.

'Well, thank you, Mr Cole,' said gold rims. 'We may need to talk to you again, but in the meantime if you should think of anything that may help us, will you contact me please.'

He held out a card. David took it tentatively. Chief Inspector Ross was printed in bold types, with an address, telephone, extension numbers and email.

'Anything at all which could give us a lead.'

'Yes, of course,' David said briskly, getting up, ready to usher them out. They seemed, somehow, to pollute the atmosphere.

As the door shut behind them, David leaned against it and shut his eyes.

'God Almighty,' he said out loud.

His reason and sanity were being surely tried. He did not believe in spirits coming back from the dead to bedevil the lives of the livings, but he now saw that the seeds of guilt and remorse sown by Michael Barlow in his last moments on earth were now reaping a rich harvest for him; Kate was dangerously ill; Fiona Moore was dead; Rob was suspected of her murder and had disappeared and Crabtree, the clairvoyant, who had supposedly been in touch with Michael's spirit was also dead.

It was a dreadful catalogue.

Michael's influence was like a cancer spreading its rot silently but viciously. At the moment he was really only on the periphery, but surely this black influence was sweeping his way and would engulf him too. It would engulf all within the circle of Michael's power.

All.

All?

That would include Timothy too.

An unnatural cold sweat broke out on David's forehead.

Timothy.

If, Kate, his wife, had not escaped, then neither would his son. These were irrational fears, he knew. Fears that a week ago he would have sneered at. But not now. Now they seemed real.

He realised that he had neglected the boy for too long. He must get in touch. He now had a terrible foreboding that the boy was in danger. He snatched up his mobile. He must ring St Austell's to see if Tim was alright.

***

Rob Moore raised the blind and looked out at the fading afternoon. A sea mist was edging in towards the promenade where an occasional ghostly pedestrian drifted by. Soon the street lights would be on and the dark would fall rapidly. Strangely, this thought disturbed him. The coming of the night made him feel uneasy. He had been struggling in the darkness so long he feared it somehow. He knew that it would always be there, waiting, ready to claim him: he was its spawn and would never be free of its grasp.

Conversely, bright light pained him. It seemed fierce and penetrating like truth, and his truth must forever lie in darkness. Oh, it was good to be alive but one had to pay a price.

He turned to look at Tim who was lying, eyes wide open, staring at the ceiling.

The boy suddenly heard his own name echo inside his head. 'Timothy,' said the voice, 'Timothy, it's time for our telephone call.'

***

He finally managed to get through to the headmaster. David Cole was not a name Mr Brett was familiar with, but when he learned the call was connected with the Barlow boy, he felt his body tense with apprehension.

'Yes, Mr Cole,' he said brightly. Too brightly.

'I am a close friend of Kate Barlow, Timothy's mother.' Despite his worry, David still felt uncomfortable in explaining his association with Kate. The headmaster apparently did not seem disposed to comment yet, as David added lamely, 'You may remember I accompanied her on her visit to the school sport's day—last June.'

'I see,' said Mr Brett.

'Well, I'm afraid that Mrs Barlow has had a car accident and has been quite badly injured.'

'I'm very sorry to hear that,' the head said slowly, not liking the turn the conversation was taking.

'At present, I don't want to bother Timothy with the news. There is nothing he can do at the moment and it would only upset him unnecessarily—but I just wanted to check that Timothy is all right—to know if he's well and healthy.'

It sounded a stupid request to make, David thought, and when there was a long pause at the other end, he thought for a moment that the head had put the phone down on him.

'Hello, Mr Brett?' he said.

'Yes, Mr Cole, I'm still here.'

'Is there a problem?'

'Oh, I'm sure there isn't. It's just that—Timothy is not in school at the present moment. He was collected this morning with his mother's permission by one of her colleagues to take part in a television show.'

'Who? Who was it?' David interrupted sharply.

'A television producer. Moore was his name. Rob Moore.'

***

Rob began to press the buttons on his mobile phone. It felt strange keying in the old familiar number. It was closer contact with the old life.

What would he do if Kate answered? He hadn't considered that. He grinned. He would do nothing—just ask to speak to David Cole.

Now the thought was planted in his thoughts, he half hoped Kate would answer the phone. To be so close to her again... to hear her voice.

But he could wait.

He knew how to be patient. As the digits clicked in some far-off exchange, he ran his fingers thorough Timothy's hair, pulling the boy closer to him as he did so.

Finally the connection was made.

The number was engaged.

***

David put the phone down slowly, his stomach constricted and his mind in a whirl of fears and fancies. He hadn't said anything to Brett about Rob being sought by the police. He would find out soon enough. He had his own problems to deal with.

And what did it all mean? Why had Rob concocted this story in order to abduct—that had to be the word for it—to abduct Timothy? Rob had never shown much interest in the boy before.

David's mind quickly re-ran the conversation they'd had the day before. Perhaps all this business about Michael and the nightmares had finally pushed him too far and he'd flipped—killed his wife and abducted the little boy. It was crazy, but in Rob's mixed up state there was no room for rationality.

These musings were interrupted by the shrill call of the telephone. Automatically, he grabbed the phone and said, 'Hello.'

There was a moment's pause then a thin piping voice came down the line to him.

'Hello, David, it's Tim.'

ELEVEN

Doctor Muncaster had just finished his examination of Kate when Sister approached him, her eyebrows arched quizzically.

'Slowly, but surely,' he said, flatly. He gave the patient another quick glance before moving on to the next room.

Through heavy-lidded eyes Kate saw swirls of white and blotches of blue, without being conscious of what it was. Without being conscious.

The darkness swelled up again and took her down again into its bleak oily embrace.

***

'Hello David. It's Tim.'

At the sound of the boy's voice, David, at first, felt a great sense of relief, which was quickly replaced by a surge of anxiety.

'Where are you, Tim? Are you all right?' he asked his mouth dry.

'Yes, I'm OK.'

His voice sounded dull and mechanical.

'Where are you?'

There was a brief pause before: 'I'm with Uncle Rob.'

David's stomach tightened. 'Is he with you now?'

There was another pause, as though the boy was checking.

'Yes.'

'Where are you, Timothy. Can you tell me?' Silence. 'Have you been hurt?'

'No.'

Thank God for that. 'Can't you tell me where you are?'

'Of course he can.' The voice had changed. It was Rob Moore.

'Rob, what the hell is all this? What are you playing at?'

'Playing? Oh Davy, boy this is for real.'

'Look, Rob, the boy's done you no harm. Please don't make things worse by hurting him.'

'Tim is fine. I have no intention of hurting him.'

'Then why not let him go?'

'I'm not forcing him to stay.'

'Where are you?'

'That's what I'm ringing about.'

David waited.

'Davy, I need to see you.'

'Yes.'

'I need to talk—face to face. Y' know about Fiona and things. You understand.'

'Of course.'

'Have the police been to see you.'

'Yes.'

'What did they say?'

Careful, David, don't frighten him away. 'They just said they wanted to see you.'

'I didn't do it, you know. I didn't cut her head off.'

David gasped. Jesus Christ, is that what happened to the poor woman? The police had not been so graphic: 'brutally murdered' they had said. Brutal indeed. Not even Rob, unbalanced as he might be, could have done that. Could he?

'I didn't kill her, I swear it.'

It sounded to David as though he were crying.

***

The lamps on the promenade now glowed feebly, yellow specks that were swallowed up by the distance and the fog.

'I didn't kill her, I swear it.' Rob Moore was saying, a broad smile crossing his face.

'Where shall we meet?' the anxious voice of David Cole reverberated on the phone.

'In thunder, lightening or in rain?' Rob smirked, but kept his voice serious. 'It's difficult, you see, David. It's got to be done

143

precisely, it's very important. You must do—exactly—what I say.'

'Go on.'

'You must come alone—without telling anyone. You promise me that?'

'Yes.'

'You promise?'

'Of course I do. I don't want to make matters worse than they already are now.'

'Good man. Very well, I want you to go into Brighton and I will meet you in the bar of the Grand Hotel. A nice crowded public place where the meeting of two old friends will not be noticed. Be there at ten o'clock. Have you got that?'

Yes, I've got it... but...'

'Good.' With a satisfied grin, Rob ended the call.

He looked out of the window at the swirling night and ruffled the hair of Timothy who was still standing limply by his side.

'Not long now, Kate, my darling. Not long now.'

***

For the headmaster of St. Austell's, watching the early evening news on television was merely a means of occupying his mind, removing his thoughts from his own cares and concerns and for thirty minutes he enjoyed seeing the trials and tribulations of others. As coloured images of industrial disputes, hi-jacks, parliamentary feuds and other social disruptions flashed before his eyes, he felt no involvement; he did not do as his favourite writer E. M. Forster encouraged—he did not connect. Instead he remained aloof and faintly satisfied with this parade of upset, chaos and misery.

The smart, urbane newsreader, it seemed, was equally, unmoved by the catalogue of human failure he presented every evening. His seriously bland expression remained intact as he relayed details of some gruesome killing in suburbia.

Wife's mutilated body found by the cleaner.

Police anxious to interview missing husband.

A face flashed on the screen. The head spilt his tea. It was a face he recognised; it was still fresh in his memory.

It was the face of Rob Moore: the man to whom he had freely given custody of one of his pupils.

He jumped up and switched the set off.

He didn't want to see it.

He didn't want to know.

And then his vision blurred briefly. That was just before he felt the tightness and the sharp fierce pain in his chest.

***

It was now dark, and the air was cold. Rob Moore shivered as he emerged from the hotel and made for the car which stood by the kerb, ghostly in the fog like a crouching beast. Quickly slipping into the driving seat, he pulled the door shut against the chill night. He was still not used to coping with the sensations of the body.

He turned the engine and with a throaty roar it burst into life. He glanced at his face in the driving mirror; it looked positively ghoulish, illuminated as it was by the dull greenish glow of the dashboard. He smiled. I won't have you for much longer, he thought to himself. It was time to dump both Rob Moore and the car; they'd both had their uses but now that usefulness was over. He wasn't quite sure where to go, but he had to be quick. Time was running out.

He moved the car forward, the fierce beams of the headlights cutting a yellow path through the misty darkness.

***

Timothy Barlow lay in the darkened room, his eyes focusing on the rectangle of light projected onto the ceiling. His brain was free of thought; his body free of feeling; even the chill of the damp room failed to make him shiver. Occasionally the rectangle of light would expand and shift as traffic passed and then his eyes would follow the movement.

The noise of Rob Moore revving up the cold car engine outside, rose loudly above all other sounds, penetrating deeply into the recesses of his mind. The noise of the car, an engine humming, throbbing, racing, the squeal of tyres.

Tim closed his eyes to darkness—to darkness and the sound of rain, rain beating against the glass. Along with this came the swish-swash of wipers as they slashed across the screen, trying to sweep aside the deluge of the rain. It was to no avail: the downpour was too heavy for the thin black arms that flickered across his line of sight. The road began to melt from view. How could he control the car? In the darkness? In the rain?

Fear grew within him. He gripped the wheel, willing the rain to stop. Rows of pin prick bright headlights grew blindingly large and then swept past him in the darkness, their spray washing across his field of vision.

And then for a moment there seemed to be respite: the rain slackened and the wipers functioned. It was to Tim like looking through wavy glass, the sort they had in the classroom doors at school. One moment you could see fairly clearly and then if you moved your head slightly your view became distorted and indistinct.

The fleeting moment of clarity allowed him to see that he was driving in the wrong lane and great beasts with yellow eyes were speeding towards him.

Desperately he swung the steering wheel over to the left and with squealing tyres, the car rocked violently and slewed across the road out of control. No problem with vision now; he could see quite clearly. He could see the hedge which was rushing towards him.

And then with some crunching and scraping, he was through it and into the blackness beyond.

Now he shivered and opening his eyes, he saw once more the rectangle of light on the ceiling.

***

146

Arthur Crabtree grinned and took her hand. 'It was all a joke, dear lady, all a joke. He isn't dead. He never was. He's just been in hiding to teach you a lesson.'

Kate snatched back her hand from the clammy grasp. 'But he is dead.'

'No. No. Not dead. Members of the jury, do you find the lady's husband dead or alive?'

The jury, all looking like Rob Moore, held up little white cards all bearing the word 'ALIVE' in black print.

'There you are, Mrs Barlow, there's nothing more to be said, is there?'

'Yes, there is.' cried a voice from the witness box. Kate turned and saw it was David, his arms firmly held by a hooded executioner.

'And what have you to say for yourself?' asked Crabtree sarcastically.

'Barlow is dead. Kate is mine now.'

The jury laughed in unison.

'My Lord, I appeal to you,' said David, turning to the bench where the judge, resplendent in red robes, sat implacably. He turned his face to David.

It was Michael.

'My dear sir,' he intoned, 'you are wasting your breath. I am alive and you are guilty of stealing my wife. The penalty is death.' He placed a black cap on his head. 'David Cole, you have been found guilty of theft and adultery and therefore you will die. In order to save time, the sentence will be carried out here and now.'

The hooded executioner raised his axe and swung it through the air sideways. Kate felt a soft breeze on her face as he did so. There then came a sickening thud and David Cole's head span through the air and landed at Kate's feet.

She gasped for air. She could hardly breathe. Her whole body writhed with horror.

'Steady. Steady.'

She blinked back the tears as she heard the voice again.

'Steady, now, Mrs Barlow.'

A face emerged through the mist of tears. A kind face. A stranger to her in a white coat.

'Welcome back to the land of the living,' it said.

***

The Keyhole Club was the second place Rob tried. The sign outside which referred to 'friendly hostesses' was what had brought him down into the converted cellar.

It was still comparatively early, and the place was fairly empty, just a few middle-aged punters dotted around the minuscule dance floor brooding over their very expensive drinks. A rough looking character who had just been approached by one of the hostesses was engaged in an animated conversation with her.

Rob wanted to do the chasing himself so, before ordering a drink, he picked the prettiest of the three girls sitting on bar stools, chatting intermittently to one another, and asked if she'd like to join him in a drink at his table. 'Of course I would,', she said. How nice. That would be lovely. She ordered for them both. The barman hoisted a bottle of champagne from under the bar. It was a familiar routine.

Rob led the way to one of the darkest corners and they sat down. After the theatrical popping of the cork, he poured the drinks and they said 'cheers'. The champagne was like vinegar, but pricey as gold.

'Mm,, that's nice,' the girl said smiling and took another gulp. She was quite a pretty thing, but pale and tired looking. She could be hardly more than twenty, he thought.

'I'm Kylie,' she said.

'Hello, Kylie, nice to know you. I'm Rob.'

'Rob. Oh that's a nice name.' Another drink. 'Is this your first time here?'

He nodded. 'It's very pleasant.'

'Yes,' she smiled and held out her glass. 'Can I have another drink?'

Make the customers spend, darling.

He poured her another vinegar juice, emptying the bottle. Surprisingly short measures in these large bottles, thought Rob.

'You're a pretty girl, Kylie.'

'Thank you, kind sir.'

'You work here full time?'

'Yes, I'm here to make your evening go with a swing.'

The practised wooden clichés sounded desperate coming from her young and tired lips.

'I bet you could really swing,' he said.

She giggled a pretend giggle. Behind that immature heavily made up face was a jaded and dispirited mind.

'You bet,' he said with a smirk. 'You make the customers feel good, eh?'

She leaned over, her thin pale hands tipped with scarlet nails touching his. 'Sure can.'

'How good?'

'Well that all depends.'

'On what?'

'Oh, on how much they want to feel good.'

'How much they can afford.'

'You could say that,' she smiled coyly.

'I just did.'

She tapped the empty bottle. 'Shall we have another bottle of bubbly?'

He frowned.

'Oh go on, Rob. I'm supposed to get you to buy another. It's part of my job,' she squeezed his hand, feeling faintly surprised how cold it was.

'You don't want to get me the sack, do you?'

'Certainly not,' he grinned, playing along with the grotesque game. 'Get you *into* the sack, maybe.'

She gave another brief giggle before holding up the empty bottle of champagne in a practised and business-like way. It was the same for her every night. This bloody pantomime: be nice to the creeps, get them to buy crap booze, then a fumble and maybe more while most of any cash that changed hands was passed over to 'the management'—or else. It was some sort of living, Kyle admitted to herself, but it was one she hated.

'Another one, Roman,' she called the barman. He nodded and within seconds was at their table with another bottle of the sour drink.

'That's Roman,' Kylie said when he had gone. 'He's from the Ukraine.'

Rob was not interested. 'Now what were we saying?'

'Oh you are eager aren't you?'

'Yes,' he said, simply.

She pursed her lips provocatively.

'What sort of pleasure do you offer?'

Suddenly her face became serious and she looked in his eyes. 'You're not a copper, are you?'

Rob laughed. It was a genuine laugh. 'No I'm not. Cross my heart and...' He stopped abruptly mid-sentence, his face losing all its animation.

'What is it?'

'Nothing,' he said coldly.

'You are telling me the truth aren't you—about being a policeman I mean?'

'Certainly am,' he smiled again, regaining his composure. 'I'm only here after pleasure.' He squeezed her arm gently. 'Or to be more accurate, now I'm after you.'

She gave a practised smile and the professional tone returned to her voice. 'Right, I can offer you relief. That'll cost you seventy five.'

'I don't want relief, sweety. I'm aiming to go the whole way.'

'Well, that'll cost you three hundred notes. In advance.'

'That's fine with me.'

'OK, dear. I have a room upstairs.'

'Ah. No. You don't understand. I want it at my place.'

She withdrew her hand. 'No dice.' The voice was hard and indifferent.

'Why not?'

She shook her head. 'It's not on. The Boss wouldn't wear it.'

'What if I doubled the fee?'

'You've got to be kidding.'

'No. You see, I can't... I can't make it except in my own bed. It's a sort of fetish I have. Come on... I'm only live five minutes drive away.'

'Six hundred quid?'

He nodded.

She pursed her lips and thought for a moment. 'Wait here. I'll see if I can fix it.'

***

Dr Anderson tapped the headmaster's chest again. The head's wife stood by watching, supported by Matron. She was ashen-faced and tearful.

Anderson shook his head. 'It looks like a massive coronary. We must get him to hospital, post haste.'

'The ambulance is on its way,' said Matron. 'I rang through for one before I contacted you.'

'Good,' he nodded grimly.

'He was just sitting, watching television.' The head's wife was slumped into a chair close to her husband. 'Just watching television,' she said again, her eyes focussing on the middle distance.

'It could happen anywhere,' said Anderson, placing a comforting arm on her shoulder. 'Even in bed.' He felt her body stiffen.

'It's this damned school,' she said bitterly. 'It's killed him.'

***

'Get in, Kylie. Your side is open.'

She did so, shivering. She had thrown on a flimsy raincoat and a scarf over her thin dress to go with him to the car.

'I hope it is only five minutes down the road,' she said, with none of the coy charm of earlier. 'I've got to be back in an hour or the boss'll give me hell.'

'That's OK. We've not got far to go.' He pulled his door shut and leaned over as though he was going to kiss her.

'Here, none of that now. I'm not doing it in a fucking freezing car if...' That was as much as she was able to say before she felt his cold hands around her neck.

'Didn't mummy warn you about men like me?' he growled, tightening his grip around her soft young flesh.

She opened her mouth to scream but no sound emerged. Her teeth gnashed together and her body erupted violently beneath him but he held firm, tightening his grasp. Soon she began to gurgle as froth collected at the corners of her mouth, her eyes widened, bulging in silent terror.

This was enjoyable. He felt great pleasure as the flesh became malleable beneath his fingers. He thrilled to feel her body tremble and gyrate against his, in the sheer desperation to escape.

But there was no escape.

Gradually, the squirming grew less and then finally the eyes, wide and protruding, ceased to move, glazed over in static, staring horror.

The girl was dead.

He pulled back to admire his handiwork, accidentally pressing the car horn with his elbow as he did so. The mournful blare into the darkness, shocked him momentarily; and then to his surprise, he noticed that he was wet with perspiration.

Time to change, he thought.

The street was empty. There was no one to see or care what was going on in the solitary vehicle with the steamed up windows.

What was going on was that Michael Barlow was transferring from an old host to a new one.

***

Kate's moments of consciousness were brief. She had only a vague notion where she was. All the consequences leading up to the why she was in hospital were lost to her. Her memory was like a granite wall; there was no getting through it or over it. Not that it concerned her. She felt relaxed—or to be more precise, overwhelmingly tired.

Kind faces had spoken comforting words to her and a swirl of activity carried on around her, but she wanted none of it. Slowly the tug of sleep became too strong and she drifted into its embrace.

***

The Michael Barlow thing looked down at its new form. If Rob Moore' body felt strange, this one certainly felt stranger. It peered through its new eyes into the driving mirror. The face that stared back was pale, heavily made up with blonde hair. She pulled her scarf around her neck, arranging it so that it hid the livid red marks on her throat. She smiled at her reflection and then glanced round at the untidy heap in the driving seat. The untidy heap that was Rob Moore.

Kylie searched through her handbag using the meagre light from the dashboard as illumination. There was little in there. Twenty pounds in cash. A packet of contraceptives, comb, lipstick, cigarette, lighter and a credit card belonging to K. White.

'So that's who I am: Kylie White' She laughed out loud with pleasure.

'Now let's put a sensible end to dear old Rob. At last you proved yourself useful, Rob old boy, so I'll see to it that you have a respectable death—to tidy things up so to speak.'

Wiping the windscreen to clear it of condensation, Kylie White checked that the street was clear before leaving the car. She quickly went round to the rear and unlocked the boot. From it she extracted a long coil of hosepipe.

She moved slowly and awkwardly at first. Perhaps it hadn't been a good idea to take on a female body with its reduced strength and unfamiliar anatomy. But the eyes twinkled at the thought that it would be most useful in deception.

She fixed one end of the hosepipe to the exhaust. It was a difficult operation to squeeze the hose over the metal rim of the blackened pipe, especially with these new hands, so long and slender. They were sensitive hands—he could learn to paint again with hands like these.

Having completed that part of the operation, Kylie White wound down the passenger window just enough for her to slip the other end of the hosepipe through and then jerked the window back up to jam it into position.

Moving around to the other side of the car, she opened the driver's door and pushed the lifeless shell of Rob Moore over into the passenger seat as she edged herself into the driving position.

At the second attempt the car started up and within moments the poisonous fumes were pumping into the car. Kylie got out and slammed the door shut.

Everything was working out very nicely. Rob's death would be seen as suicide. Remorse and despair at having killed his wife had driven him to it. Kylie smiled; 'driven' was rather an apt word. The suicide would be accepted without question—there would be no mystery concerning either his death or his wife's. There would be no loose ends. No complications that could cause problems when he was back with Kate.

Kate.

There was only David Cole to deal with now and then he could be finally re-united with her.

Kate.

Kylie White shivered as a gust of wind blew down the street. Pulling the raincoat closer to, she turned and moved off quickly into the night.

She had a very important appointment to keep.

TWELVE

The elegant Victorian Bar of the Grand Hotel in Brighton was not crowded as Rob had suggested it might be. Out of season, the hotel relied on businessmen as weekday clients and only a few of these were seated in the long narrow bar room. One or two were alone studying their mobiles, missing their wives or girlfriends. In the conservatory beyond, overlooking the promenade, were a group of tired-looking executives obviously talking shop. All very normal and mundane. How many times in his life had David sneered at the normal and mundane? Now he would welcome them with open arms.

He perched on one of the leather stools at the far end of the bar so that he could see everyone who came in. He asked the barman for a large whisky and nibbled a few peanuts subconsciously while he waited for it.

He glanced at his watch. 9.50. Ten minutes to go. He took a long drink, the whisky burning the back of his throat. It was good. He enjoyed the discomfort of it.

The alcohol began to relax him and then he thought about Kate.

He'd been to see her at the hospital again before coming here. There had been some change. The Sister said that she had regained consciousness for a while and then slipped into a more natural sleep. It sounded good, but this information was delivered in such dour, flat tones that he didn't know what to think. He certainly wasn't uplifted by the news; the Sister's manner only fuelled his anxiety.

However, the fact that Kate had been moved to a side ward had seemed a hopeful sign, and he tried to cheer himself up with this; but the cold night, the uncertainty of his errand and, fierce gut-pummelling reality had dissipated any easing of the depression he felt.

He had stayed some fifteen minutes gazing down at Kate's still form. Despite the bruises, she still looked beautiful; that fine delicate nose and that wide sensuous mouth. He longed to see her grey intelligent eyes again bright and sparkling with life. Watching her, he had cried a little. Somehow he felt—knew—deep down that she would never come back to him. It could never be as it was before. And at the same time, he sensed something dying within him, too.

He pulled himself back to the present, cursing each morbid thought that clouded his brain. He took another drink. While she was alive there was hope. Hold on to that thought.

Ten o'clock came and went. There was no sign of Rob. God, I hope this isn't some kind of hoax and he isn't going to turn up. Why on earth would he drag me here if he had no intention of meeting me? David's scriptwriter brain began to work on this conundrum. Perhaps, he mused, it is not so much that he wants me here, he just doesn't want me at the cottage.

Out of the way.

What for? And why had he taken Tim? Was he really telling the truth when he swore that he didn't kill Fiona? Questions, questions. Who the hell can find the answers with his twisted mentality? It was pointless trying to reason what he would do. Reason did not come into it.

Ten fifteen and no Rob.

David's stomach began to churn. If he really did kill his wife, what wild things might he be doing now? At this moment. He should have told the police. In fact, he wasn't really sure why he hadn't. Some vague feelings of loyalty to Rob, maybe. But how can you be loyal to a mad man?

Sitting quietly in these pleasant surroundings with a drink, which was easing the tension within him, he could see quite clearly now that he had been a fool. He downed the last of his whisky. Time I went, he told himself.

'David.'

Someone close to him spoke his name, softly but very clearly.

He turned to face the speaker. To his surprise he saw that it was a young woman in her early twenties. She was thin, blonde-haired and heavily made-up, but fairly attractive in an obvious way.

'David Cole?'

'Yes,' he replied tentatively.

'I'm Kylie White.' She looked around cautiously. 'I'm a friend of Rob's.'

'Oh!' David did not like this at all. He had never seen or heard of the girl before and she certainly didn't look like Rob's type one bit.

'He's asked me to meet you and take you back to him.' She spoke softly, her brown eyes furtively scanning the bar. 'He felt he couldn't risk being seen in public.'

'I see.'

'So if you'll come now, I'll take you to him.'

'Where is he?'

'He asked me not to say in case I was overheard.'

'By whom, for Christ's sake?' David spoke the words softly but they resonated with his frustrated anger. 'If I'm being followed, they'll follow wherever you're taking me.'

Kylie's bottom lip began to tremble.

'Don't make me break my promise to Rob, please.'

David gave a heavy sigh of resignation. 'OK. Come on.'

'We'll need to take your car.'

'Right.' he said leaving his stool. 'Let's get this over with.'

'Thank you, David,' she said, taking his arm as they left the bar.

***

The Scottish nurse took Kate's pulse. She wasn't pleased with it. In the pale glow of the bedside lamp, Kate's face appeared waxy and unnaturally still. The fact that she hadn't stopped breathing was evident from her slow pulse rate, but other than that she had all the appearance of a corpse.

The nurse knew peaceful, restful sleep, but this she felt was not it. Mrs Barlow gave all the signs of great surrender.

It fitted a grim pattern she knew well: the brief encouraging rally before the inevitable.

She turned on her heel and hurried from the room to find Sister.

***

On Kylie White's instructions, David pulled up outside one of the hotels in the less salubrious end of Brighton. Outside in the misty gloom of the night he could just make out the words on the illuminated sign: Ocean Vis a Hotel.

'Rob's waiting for us in there,' said Kylie . 'Shall we go in?'

Ironically enough, David considered this rather dramatic cloak and dagger scenario typical of Rob Moore. Arranging to meet him and then simply keeping the appointment was too straightforward for Rob. There had to be complications and convolutions: they were his stock in trade. Therefore, it was with no real sense of unease that David complied with Kylie's suggestion.

They moved quickly through the foyer to the lift. A small Asian man was at the reception desk and he hardly gave them a glance. The cramped stale-smelling lift shook and rattled its way to the third floor and then Kylie led him along a dimly lit corridor.

'This is it,' she said when they at last reached the room and unlocking the door she bade David enter. 'Go on in.'

David did so. The room was in darkness but broad shafts of light fell through the window on to one of the two beds inside. Lying on the bed, perfectly still but with eyes wide open staring at the ceiling was Timothy Barlow.

'Tim. Thank God!' cried David, making a move towards the boy. A light snapped on flooding the room with harsh light and he heard a voice behind him.

'He's resting; leave him alone.'

The resonance and the quality of the voice stopped David in his tracks. It was a voice that was somehow familiar and yet it sounded strangely alien—unearthly. He turned round and there was no one there. No one except for Kylie White leaning against the closed door.

She smiled.

'Hello, David.'

The voice, this strange guttural voice, was coming from her.

'What's going on? Where's Rob?'

'Don't concern yourself about Rob. He's never going to bother anyone again.'

'What do you mean? Who are you?'

'Inquisitive, aren't we?'

The voice was changing, subtly at first, deepening in pitch and growing more familiar.

Too familiar.

A fierce chill invaded David's body. Surely it couldn't be?

'Yes, my friend, you recognise this voice, don't you? It's the one that pierces your nightmares. You are not mistaken. I am Michael. I have returned. As I said I would.'

The female creature raised her arms. 'Oh, I know this body is unfamiliar to you but don't let that distract you from the truth. After all it is only a temporary arrangement.'

David closed his eyes and shook his head violently. Either he was going mad, his brain slipping into dark world of insanity— or it really was happening.

'I have been waiting, longing to return, return to my darling Kate and to settle a few scores. There was you and there was Rob who required punishment. I needed to settle those debts. And it was that little medium fellow Crabtree that provided, the pathway, the portal through which I could return. And here I am.' The Michael creature opened its mouth wide in a deep guttural laugh.

'You… you killed Fiona Moore. It was you.'

'Indeed. And Rob.'

'Rob.'

'Yes, your old buddy is dead too. I used his body for a while. But I needed to move on. As I do now.'

This last statement made David shudder; but in doing so he finally accepted the horrifying and insane truth of it all. And with this acceptance came strength. It was as though he had passed through a doorway of understanding into another realm of consciousness. He was facing a new reality and with this he suddenly felt stronger within himself. He had to believe the impossible; accept this fantastic scenario. Only by doing so could he take action and survive. Here then before him in the shape of a frail young woman was Michael Barlow—back from the dead. Strangely, it now all seemed possible, even logical. He had been fighting this nightmare for long enough with reason and rationality and they had failed. Now he had to face the truth, however incredible.

Yes, Michael Barlow was back from the dead.

Rob had known. He had been aware of this power that reached out from the grave to touch the lives of the living.

Now he knew. Now he believed.

The full implication of this dark truth flooded his body with warmth and strength like a hidden power. Doubt and tiredness were swept aside and he felt his frame glow with an inner freedom. It was a blessed release.

He made a move towards the creature masquerading as Kylie White, but her eyes flashed and their piercing gaze held him back.

'Don't do that, Cole. It's useless. I am in total control. Resign yourself to that fact. You are mine to do with as I will.'

Timothy, who had been quiet and still up to this moment, suddenly gave out a long, agonised moan and stirring feverishly, he raised himself slightly from the bed.

David turned to the boy with concern, forgetting momentarily his own danger. 'Tim, Tim,' he called. 'Are you all right?'

The boy's eyes flickered wildly, and he called out softly.

'Mother,' he said.

For a fleeting moment, it seemed as though he knew David. His features brightened with the recognition, before the lids closed down and he slumped back in apparent unconsciousness.

'He wants Kate and so do I,' said the Michael creature.

'Do you?' David turned to Kylie White. He was vibrating with anger now; his head pounded with his own fury. He no longer felt afraid; just angry—bitterly angry.

'If you want Kate you had better hurry up and do whatever you have to—if you want her before she dies.'

Kylie White looked shocked. Her face blanched, the features mirroring the turmoil of emotion the creature felt at what David had said. Disbelief and fear fought for mastery of expression.

'You lie.' The words were spat out.

'Do I? You bastard.' David replied with matching vehemence. 'It's because of you... It's because of you that she's dying. She crashed her car after the damned séance.'

David had the bleak satisfaction of seeing this creature visibly shrink at this revelation. He carried on, twisting the knife in the wound, giving full vent to his anger.

'She's in Intensive Care at St. Luke's. It is only a matter of time before she dies.' He said the last sentence slowly and coolly placing emphasis on each word.

The figure of Kylie White staggered backwards and as it crashed into the door an agonised inhuman cry of torment issued from its lips. As the cry vibrated in the stillness of the room, Timothy Barlow roused himself once more, calling out for his mother. David crossed to him.

'Leave him,' the creature snarled, the Kylie White face contorted in fury. 'Leave my son alone.'

David turned to face the Michael thing, and once more its fiery red eyes fixed him with their penetrating gaze and held him. It was as though he were paralysed; he could not move a muscle.

'Kate will not die,' it said in a deep guttural croak. 'I have not come back in order to let my darling Kate die. I need your body for my own.'

David struggled to move, but those fierce eyes dominated him. They glowed like burning coals; he could feel their power penetrating his mind.

'Think of the bitter poetic justice, Cole, when I make love to Kate with your body.'

***

All was quiet in the ward. Nurse Gillis was just about to go and make herself a hot drink when there was a scream. It seemed to ricochet against the walls and fill the whole ward with noise. At first she couldn't place the scream—actually now, she realised, it was more of a cry.

Then she knew where it came from.

She ran into Kate's room to find her sitting bolt upright in bed. She was calling someone's name at the top of her voice. Was it Jim? No, Tim. That was it, Tim.

***

'Think of the bitter irony,' the creature was saying, 'when I make love to Kate with your body.'

Without warning Tim leapt from the bed and flung himself straight at Kylie. The creature, caught completely by surprise, was knocked sideways by the ferocity of the boy's attack. Tim's fingers were scratching and gouging at Kylie's face and she lost her balance altogether and crashed to the ground with the boy sitting astride her.

David took one step forward to assist, but Tim called out to him.

'No, David. Go. Run. Get out of here or he'll kill you.'

David faltered. The words were true and he knew it. This Michael creature would surely not harm his own son, but he had no such immunity. His death was not only a necessity but it would give Michael pleasure. This was his chance to escape: he could not miss it.

Sidestepping the fallen girl who was still struggling with the frenzied boy, he grasped the door handle, flung the door open and fled the room.

Seeing David escape, Kylie White emitted a ferocious roar of fury and with strength not natural for the frail female body, she rose from her prone position and lifted Tim above her head. Without hesitation, she flung him across the room. With a whistling intake of breath, the boy crashed against the wall above his bed. There was a sharp snap and twist of the neck, as he fell, landing awkwardly on the floor.

The sudden stillness of his body shocked the Michael creature and its boiling fury died instantly. Her long, thin nervous fingers reached out and touched the face of the inert figure. She ran them gently down Tim's cheek and slowly on to his neck. There was no doubt about it: it was broken.

Pain and anguish ripped through its very being and the Kylie White body crumpled to the floor with an unearthly wail.

***

David stumbled out into the icy night air. How his feet carried him down the stairs and through the hotel foyer, he did not know; he was just glad to be out of the place and breathing good fresh air. As he hurried into the street, his feet slipped on the wet surface and he fell to the ground, his hands scraping along the cold, slimy pavement. The sudden shock and pain helped to clear his muddled mind a little. He knew that whatever that thing was back there in the hotel room, it was evil and he had to get away from it. For the moment, little else mattered.

However, as he pulled himself to his feet, his head began to throb, filling with strange sounds. They filtered in at first, insidious and faint, but then they grew in volume, until the noise became painful. Wincing with the increasing racket in his head, he tried to carry on walking, but the thunderous throb played havoc with his co-ordination. Like a man learning to walk with artificial limbs, he thrust one leg forward. The knee gave way and he staggered forward almost colliding with an elderly couple who were passing by. They quickly dodged out of his way, staring disapprovingly at him. The man said something but David could only make out the word 'drunk'.

He didn't care. He could hardly think: his head roared with the noise. It was like the booming of drums. The heavy beat thundered in his brain.

Thundered.

Thundered.

THUNDERED.

He dragged himself unsteadily towards his car, the noise drawing all the energy from him so that he could hardly lift one foot after another. Each step required all his concentration and effort. He fought desperately to maintain his equilibrium, but incredibly, the drumming grew louder, drowning his reason in a flood of noise. Each step took a lifetime and when eventually he reached the car, he did not fully comprehend what he was doing. It was only reflex action which caused him to pull the car keys from his coat. He looked down at them, shining dimly in his hand. He fumbled with them, his fingers testing the silver shapes until he found the one he wanted. With infinite slowness, his mind fighting against the power of the noise, he inserted it into the lock, turned it and heard the satisfying clunk as the central locking system released itself. Still functioning on some inbuilt automatic pilot, his trembling hands grasped the door handle. It was slimy and cold to the touch. With a feverish effort he pulled the car door open and fell onto the driver's seat.

***

'Well?' said the sister, softly, her brows inquisitively.

The doctor shook his head, his eyes remaining impassive. 'There's nothing we can do now.'

Poor woman, thought the sister. Poor woman.

***

The thunder continued.

David was now ready to surrender to it completely.

And then... through the misted haze of the windscreen he saw the figure of Kylie White emerge from the hotel. The cold hand of fear grasped him so tightly that it shocked him into action. He had never been so frightened in his life.

He pulled himself up in the driver's seat and began fumbling with his car keys again in a desperate search for the ignition key.

God, I must get away, his mind screamed over the cacophony in his brain. I must get away from that thing. I must. He found the key: the shiny sliver of metal that would help him escape. The drums thundered on. At any moment his head would burst open.

Like a drunken man, he aimed the key at the ignition switch. It wouldn't go in. The key was now enormous—far too big for the slot he was trying to slip it into.

He looked up in panic and saw Kylie White gazing into the street. Her eyes flashed with demonic intensity. She glanced in his direction. God, she had seen him.

His hand gripped the key so tightly that it pierced his skin.

'Get in, you bastard!' he cried, once more trying to push it into the ignition.

A fierce smile brushed Kylie's lips as she moved down the hotel steps towards the car.

The key skidded past the slot again.

'Damn you,' he yelled.

He tried once more, the tip of the key wavered over the aperture and quickly he rammed it home.

'Thank God.' Swiftly he turned the ignition. The engine, cold and damp as it was, protested noisily at this rough attempt to start it.

Kylie White was moving slowly with deliberation towards the car.

David tried again. This time the engine turned and then reluctantly spluttered into life. In mad triumph David yelled a cry of delight, almost drowning the noise in his head.

Kylie was nearly at the car now, her face appearing hideous, illuminated by the headlights and distorted by the condensation on the windows.

David whipped the handbrake off and put his foot down. The engine roared lustily and then died in a choking splutter. Like a demented man, his mouth working noiselessly, fingers working in spasms, David turned the ignition key again.

Kylie now had her hand on the door.

The engine hummed.

He jammed his foot down on the accelerator.

Kylie pulled the passenger door open.

Tyres squealed and the car leapt forward, wrenching the door from her grasp.

With a furious passion, David drove away at high speed, the car rocking wildly, the door still swinging open.

Through the mirror he could see the lone static figure of Kylie White staring after him. She rapidly grew smaller until she disappeared into the distance.

After driving for about a mile, he felt it safe enough to stop and close the open door. This done, he drove on, he knew not where just as long as it was away from that creature. The further he drove the quieter the drums sounded in his head until after a few miles or so, the noise faded away completely. It was then that he pulled over to the grass verge, his body drenched in sweat and his hands still shaking with fear. He slumped over the wheel exhausted in mind and body.

Unconsciousness, like a pleasing wine seeped into his body and he fell into the arms of a deep and merciful sleep.

***

Some thirty minutes later a taxi drew up outside St. Luke's hospital and a slim blonde in a thin raincoat got out. After paying the driver she hurried inside to the enquiry desk.

'It's my sister, Kate Barlow. She's in Intensive Care, I believe. I've only just heard about it: I've been out of the country for a while.' The words were spilled out in an emotional flood. It was a convincing performance.

'Just a moment, love.' The night porter put down his paperback and wandered off into a back room.

Kylie White turned away and leaned with her back against the counter. Her face was devoid of expression, but inside the shell of this girl, the Michael-creature was coiled and tense.

'Yes. She's in Intensive Care, love.' The porter had returned. 'Apparently she's been moved into a private side ward.'

'Oh. Is that good or bad?'

The porter looked at her, his tired face forming a non-committal smile, 'Difficult to say, love. It usually means they're on the mend.' He leaned over the counter and pointed. 'You go down this corridor to the end; then turn right and you'll see the lift. That'll take you up to Intensive.'

'Thank you.'

Kylie White hurried away down the corridor.

The porter returned to the paperback, mumbling to himself. 'It usually means they're on the mend—or there's nothing more they can do for 'em.'

***

David awoke.

He was conscious of the cold and the dark. As he focused his eyes on the blackness before him, the glare of the brilliant yellow light filled his line of vision and then in an instant was gone.

And then there came another.

And another.

Headlights.

Slowly his mind cleared and his memory began to function. Fragments from the past few days and mental snapshots gradually fell into place and he remembered. He remembered everything and shuddered.

For him, in the last twenty-four hours the world had gone mad. Nothing seemed real any more. Somehow he had been spirited away into another reality—a world where dead men walked, inhabiting the bodies of the living.

David put his head in his hands and emitted a long low grieving moan. What was he to do? Dear God, what was he to do? Suddenly, the answer came to him: clear and obvious. He had to get to Kate before Michael did. The thought came with such searing clarity that without further hesitation, he started up the car. He must get to Kate before Michael. He didn't know why; he just knew that he had to.

***

'There's no record of Mrs Barlow having a sister.'

Kylie White did not reply at first. She just stared defiantly at the nurse. And then she said with quiet deliberation: 'I would hardly be here at this time of night to visit a stranger. May I see my sister now?' Her face remained an expressionless mask.

Nurse Gillis felt intimidated but poor Kate Barlow was dying and she could hardly deny access to this woman who ever she may be. She nodded to the woman and said: 'Come this way, please. We've moved her into a side ward for more privacy.'

As the nurse turned, she felt a restraining hand on her arm.

'Tell me,' said the woman, 'Is she dying? The truth, please.'

The nurse hesitated a moment before attempting a reply, but the expression on her face answered the query more eloquently than words.

Kylie White gave a guttural croak and seemed to stagger back against the wall.

'Are you all right?' asked the nurse but the woman did not reply. She just leant against the wall for some moments, her eyes glazed and vacant as though she were in some kind of trance. And then quite abruptly she seemed to snap out of it and pull herself together.

'Please take me to my sister.'

Nurse Gillis led her to Kate. In the dimly lit room, she was lying on her back with her arms placed by her side outside the smoothed down white covers. The pale sunken face, framed by dark hair was just visible over the crisp sheet, tucked neatly under her chin. The features were at rest: the eyes were closed.

'Leave me,' said Kylie White. The words though spoken softly were imperious and harsh.

The nurse left.

Kylie White knelt down by the bed, her face close to Kate's.

'Kate. Wake up. It's me. Michael. I said I would come back, didn't I? Well, here I am.' The words were a whisper—a dark penetrating whisper in masculine tones. Pulling back the cover, the creature took Kate's hand and squeezed it. 'Kate, don't give in now. Don't desert me at the last. It's Michael, I've come back for you.' Kylie White felt the pulse rate quicken slightly.

'Kate, my darling: Wake up. Fight against the darkness; don't let it take you.'

Gently and erratically the eyelids fluttered and then with infinite slowness they opened.

'Kate, I've come back to you, just like I said I would.'

The forehead furrowed as the eyes tried to focus. Those sensuous lips parted slightly and the tip of her tongue trailed along the contours in a feeble attempt to moisten them. The pupils of her eyes dilated and retracted trying to bring the room into focus. Gradually they steadied and she seemed to see the figure before her.

'Kate,' it said.

It was a voice she knew.

That voice.

It repeated her name again.

Her eyes widened.

'Michael?' she said, her voice barely audible.

'Yes, my darling. I've come back for you. I'll never leave you again.'

Her glazed eyes widened further. Incredulity and horror were mirrored in there.

'Don't you worry about how I look. I'll soon change that. What matters is that I'm back for good.'

Kate gave a gagging sound in her throat and with all her feeble strength she raised herself a few inches from the bed, her mouth working violently in desperation to say something. But no words came.

Finally, she fell back against the pillow.

It took some moments for the Michael-creature to realise that Kate was dead.

***

As David approached the hospital, he could see a small group of people gathered on the path by the shrubbery to the left of the main entrance. Drawing nearer he saw that the object of their interest was a body sprawled halfway on the path and half in the shrubbery. Pushing his way closer, his heart missed a beat as he recognised the thin yellow dress the corpse was wearing.

It was the body of Kylie White.

She was sprawled awkwardly on the ground like a discarded doll; her body lay in the shrubbery but her head had caught the stone pathway and had cracked open. Blood and brains lay glistening by the doll-like face—a face that was barely recognisable.

'What happened?' he asked.

'Looks like she fell from one of the windows up there?' said a burly fellow dressed in a heavy overcoat. He pointed upwards.

David gazed up at the row of lighted windows like yellow eyes staring out at the night and noticed one which was open, the white net curtain gently flapping in the breeze.

'How she came to do it, I don't know,' the same fellow was saying.

'It must be suicide,' said another bystander.

At that moment a doctor and two orderlies carrying a stretcher emerged from the hospital and the group of onlookers moved back. David glanced up at the open window again, mentally counting the floors. As he did so, he saw the window close.

While the orderlies lifted the remains of Kylie White onto the stretcher, David ran past them into the hospital. Within minutes he was ringing the bell on the Intensive Care Ward.

'Come on. Come on,' he snarled with impatience.

The door was opened by Nurse Gillis.

'I must see Kate Barlow.'

'Yes, of course.'

He brushed past her and went into Kate's room.

Kate was lying still, on her back, her arms resting on top of the white covers. She looked at peace.

As he moved towards the bed, he noticed that the net curtain had been trapped in the window when it had been closed. His mind was distracted from this observation by some movement in the bed.

Kate stirred and opened her eyes.

She smiled. It was a sweet smile.

David was speechless looking down at her. At her pale smiling face. And those eyes.

Those eyes.

Somehow they seemed strange.

They held none of Kate's familiar warmth.

And yet he knew those eyes.

He had seen that satisfied stare before.

He had gazed at it in a painting.

Then he knew.

As he finally realised the awful truth, his heart turned to ice. The eyes in that smiling face still continued to gaze at him. Michael had achieved his ultimate desire. He was now as close to Kate as he could ever be.

'Come to me, David.' Kate said, smiling sweetly.

David wanted to scream.

Printed in Great Britain
by Amazon

19796900R00109